LAndmarked
for
Murder

Sisters in Crime / Los Angeles Chapter

Top Publications, Ltd.
Dallas, Texas

LAndmarked for Murder

A Top Publications Paperback

First Edition

Top Publications, Ltd.
12221 Merit Drive, Suite 950
Dallas, Texas 75251

ISBN#: 0-9666366-37-2

Library of Congress Control Number 2006906706

Printed in the United States of America

LAndmarked
for
Murder

Contents

Foreword
by Taylor Smith

This latest anthology of short mystery stories by the Los Angeles Chapter of Sisters in Crime comes just as the national organization is celebrating its twentieth anniversary.

Sisters in Crime was founded in 1986 by Sara Paretsky and friends. Their aim: *"To combat discrimination against women in the mystery field, educate publishers and the general public as to inequities in the treatment of female authors, raise the level of awareness of their contributions to the field, and promote the professional advancement of women who write mysteries."*

Now, twenty years on, you may wonder whether the organization hasn't outlived its usefulness—fallen victim to its own success. You only have to browse the mystery section of your favorite bookstore to see how many works by talented female authors stand side by side next to those of their similarly talented brethren.

And yet... and yet...

I spent the past five years coordinating a national project to monitor mystery book reviews in newspapers, periodicals and, more recently, online portals. The aim of the project: to gauge whether female and male authors were getting equal print attention.

It's not just about vanity. P.T. Barnum said that "all publicity is good publicity." In publishing, there's a direct correlation between reviews and sales. The more attention a book gets, the more buyers line up to see what all the fuss is about.

When Sisters in Crime was founded twenty years ago, there was a gut level feeling women mystery authors were getting short shrift. In order to quantify that, the Review Monitoring Project was created. Forty-some monitors across the country have been tracking mystery reviews in their neck of the woods, feeding hard numbers to the National Coordinator (who was me from 2000-2005; Judy Clemens from Ohio has now taken over). What we've discovered is that in some markets—a very few—there's near parity. In most, however, reviews devoted to male authors way outstrip the number for female authors.

Why? There are various possible reasons. Maybe it's the gender of the reviewers—traditional wisdom says men won't read books by women, but that women will read both male and female authors. Also, paperbacks are rarely reviewed, so if women authors are over-represented in paperback and under-represented in hardback originals, that could be part of the problem. Some people also believe that women authors are all writing "chick-lit" style stories with more limited reader appeal. You only have to read some of the grittier stuff in this anthology to know that ain't necessarily so.

The Los Angeles chapter of Sisters in Crime, like all 48 chapters worldwide, counts men as well as women among its 3400 very talented members. What you hold in your hands is a sampling of some of the best short fiction produced this past year by those L.A.-based Sisters—and Brothers—in Crime. I can't think of a better way to remind ourselves that a flair for great storytelling comes in all kinds of packages.

So, Happy Anniversary, *Sisters in Crime*! And Happy Reading, mystery fans.

Taylor Smith,
author of the forthcoming *Slim to None* and numerous other thrillers

INTRODUCTION: 100 SUBURBS IN SEARCH OF A CITY
by Susan K. Beery

Why a mystery anthology set around L.A. landmarks? Landmarks define a city. They are more than fixed objects that mark a location. They are mirrors that reflect our history, monuments to human triumph and tragedy. A single landmark can transcend its original purpose, and slip into our collective consciousness as a political symbol, a pop icon, or a memorial to unspeakable horror and death. Importantly, landmarks cut across cultural barriers to draw people from all strata, and for the mystery writer, that opens up a world of deadly possibilities.

While London has Big Ben, Paris has the Eiffel Tower, Sydney has the Opera House, and Athens has the Parthenon (to name a few), Los Angeles is too big and too diverse for a single landmark. We are a mosaic of neighborhoods populated by a crazy quilt of cultures. Yes, there are the naysayers who claim L.A. has no history, as if a fully formed modern city had somehow sprung whole from the head of Zeus. Obviously, they don't know the Los Angeles we live in, and write about.

In the stories that follow, you'll journey to all corners of Los Angeles, and visit ten of our famous and infamous landmarks. Some you already know, some you may have forgotten, and some you will view in a chilling new light. The excursion is free, but reader, be warned. Desperation blows through the San Gabriel Valley on the back of a hot Santa Ana wind. Greed walks the carpeted halls of downtown hotels. Terror stalks the college campus. Fear floats in the Venice Canals, and at Santa Anita Race Track jealousy runs in the eighth. And that's only a few of the treacherous stops.

The Landmark Express is about to depart...and murder is about to bubble up, blacker than the La Brea Tar Pits. Climb aboard for the ride, if you dare...

*South Dakota may have Mount Rushmore, but Los Angeles has the **Eagle Rock**, a mountain-size rock with an eagle in flight etched into its face. Here, along its windswept ridge, we begin our murderous tour of L.A. landmarks. The forces of nature—wind, rain, and erosion, have all lent a hand in creating this natural landmark, which became the namesake for the L.A. community of Eagle Rock. The reddish-brown Rock's colorful history is the stuff of legends. Centuries ago, the Native Americans used it as a natural fort. The Spanish called it La Piedra Gorda, 'fat rock.' Stories still told today in the local cafés recall the bandit Tiburcio Vásquez who, in 1874, used the Rock as a hideout during his robbery spree. Then there was the alcoholic French beekeeper who lived in one of Eagle Rock's two caves. For our tour, a bit of advice— watch where you step and always look over your shoulder…*

LEAVING SLACKERLAND
by Gay Degani

I trip along the ridge from my apartment, Usher on my iPod, cell phone off, feeling blessedly lit. All I want to do is lie in the dirt next to the Eagle Rock, watch the stars, and celebrate the end of my screwed-up life. That dumbshit Tommy Royle, or as he likes to call himself "T-Royal," just dumped me. And I'm pumped. Tommy got me so caught up, I couldn't break up with him. Kept thinking I'd do it tomorrow, later, whenever, but "whenever" never came. Now it's done. No more slacker boyfriends for me. Not after Kevin, not after Dustin, Jason, Yegor, and especially not after Tommy. I'm so over it.

When I hit the clearing, I do a little dance and glance down the cement steps built into the side of the hill. Making sure old Tommy isn't down in the park doing one of his quick deals. But there on the steps...what is that? A walrus? At least I think it's a walrus, right by the fallen oak, staring straight at me. I blink, unbelieving, and take a quick peek over my shoulder. Yep, the ocean's still where it's supposed to be, a good twenty miles away, the orange sun dipping behind the LA skyline. I look back at the lump. Squint. Still see the faint gleam of tusks. Maybe the tequila was a bad idea. And the Xanax chaser.

Picking my way down the crumbling stairs, I figure

the beast isn't real, just an alcohol-induced illusion. When I reach out, when I touch it, my hand snaps back. My stomach tenses. Whatever it is, it's warm and solid.

I step around the tree for a closer look. The dirt gives way under my foot. I start to fall. Grab for a tusk. It comes with me. I scream, but the tusk holds. I scramble up, rock and dirt slipping and scraping my knees, and pitch myself onto the other side of the rotted trunk, earphones flying.

Spitting out grit, I open my eyes. Try to focus. The tusks morph into pale white legs hanging over the fallen tree. The walrus, the tree itself. No. I push away, but I have to look. Blonde hair drapes the stairs. The form begins to take shape. A woman. A gaping hole where her neck ought to be. When I realize who it is, I pass out.

I wake to a steady rush of traffic on the 134. Tangles of branches sway above my head. Shit. I'll never drink again. I shiver and turn.

The eyes of Chloe Moss meet mine. Flat, accusing. Dead. No. Not dead. Can't be, yet only a thin glimmer of skin seems to connect her white face to the rest of her body. I swallow the sour taste in my mouth, bolt up, and vomit on my jeans. Shaking, dizzy, I wipe my mouth. And that's when I see it. Lifted to my face, clutched in my own right hand, is a gun. I drop it. BANG...it goes off.

Sweating now, I listen for running feet, any sign that someone's coming. The six or seven houses overlooking the ravine are within earshot. But all I hear is a lone dump truck leaving the Scholl Canyon landfill.

I gape at Chloe, her eyes spooky, wide open and fixed. Should I check her pulse? Scream for help? Call 911? I pat the waistband of my pants, scramble around in the dirt, but my cell phone's gone. I draw my legs up under my chin; bite hard on my bottom lip. Can't move. Can't think. Tremble instead because this is not just any dead body. Chloe Moss is the reason T-Royal broke up with me.

Then a siren shrieks somewhere behind me. My fingernails dig into my palms. The pain wakes me. Move. Run.

Back in my apartment, my aunt's apartment until she died on me, I dig out an old duffle. Toss in toothbrush, curling iron...forget the curling iron...jeans, T-shirts, the bottle of José Gold and all the prescription pills Tommy's ordered off the Internet and stored in my freezer. Fucking Tommy. What did he say to me on the phone just a while ago?

Asshole: "We're over. I got someone else."

Me: "That bitch Chloe?"

Asshole: "It's complicated."

What's so complicated, Tommy T-Royal? That's what I thought at the time. Now she's dead, the kind of complication that calls for heavy pharmaceuticals.

* * *

By the time I pull my Jetta onto the grass in Tujunga—three beaters crowd the driveway—it's ten o'clock at night.

Kevin's girlfriend Holly answers the door with a brat on her hip. She looks me up and down, frowns. I'd met her before at a rave where Tommy slipped Kevin some Ecstasy. Free of charge. Showing Kevin how pimp he is. Knowing Kevin and I'd been tight.

Taking a drag on her cigarette, Holly says, "He's

sleeping. Can't you hear him snoring?"

"Can I come in?"

"Don't you have a mother?"

"She's not that kind of mother."

I stick out my chin, straighten my shoulders, daring her to slam the door. Holly shifts the kid to the other hip, says, "What're you standing out there for? You're letting in all the cold air."

The next morning Kevin leans over me on the couch and says, "Hey, Pep-Squad." He's all bristly beard and bad breath.

"I'm in big trouble," I say.

"Knocked up again?"

"No-o-o." I smack him hard on the shoulder, annoyed, hurt. Punch him again and again. He wraps his arms around me, and I cry a little.

Later I tell them what happened. We're sitting at the cluttered dinette table on rusty metal chairs. Kevin sucks on a bong. Sixteen-month-old Isabel peers at me from her mother's lap with a string of drool on her chin, while Holly, lines already stitched around her lips, blows cigarette smoke from her nose. I think, she could be me. If I hadn't miscarried.

"Nikki." Kevin snaps his fingers in my face. I gape at him. There's probably drool on my chin too. "So the killer hid in the bushes and when you passed out, he put the gun in your hand?"

"That's what happened."

"Turn yourself in," says Holly.

Kevin gives her a dirty look, then says to me, "Where's the gun?"

"I threw it down the hill."

He pushes his chair out and walks to the refrigerator, grabs a carton of orange juice, and gulps. His Adam's apple bumps up and down. I glance at Isabel, her face scrunched up, shaking her head, trying to avoid her mother's smog. "Can I take her?"

Holly hands her over. "Go to the police, Nik. You didn't do anything wrong except find a body. I know a cop at the Eagle Rock Station. He'll know what to do."

"Forget it. That guy's a dick," says Kevin. "Mexico's the place. Ensenada. Cabo. I'll give you one of my cars. Who was this Cleo person anyway?"

"Her name's Chloe. Tommy and I met her at the A & D Club a couple of weeks ago. I knew something was up between them, but it took a while to figure it out."

"This doesn't look good," says Kevin. "This ho steals your boyfriend and now she's dead."

"So what?" says Holly. "Nikki didn't do it. Running away makes it look like she did."

"It *already* looks like she did."

They really go at it now, so I slip into the bedroom and put Isabel in her crib. "Shh, little girl. I'd take you with me, but I am so freakin' screwed." I wipe her watery eyes with a tissue and hand her a stuffed Minnie Mouse. "Keep your head down, Iz."

Kevin and Holly are still shouting in the kitchen. I tiptoe into the living room, snatch my duffle from the sofa, and split.

I'm starting the Jetta when Kevin sprints out of the house. "Pep-squad," he calls.

I stop and wait. "Give it up on the 'Pep-squad,' Kevin.

I got kicked off, remember?"

"Yeah, yeah. But, hey, don't listen to Holly. She doesn't know anything." I begin to crank up the window, but he grabs the glass. "Wait. Does Royle have a gun?"

"I don't know. Maybe. His father has guns." I've been thinking about this, trying to keep it under my own radar.

"But you've never seen a gun?"

"I don't think Tommy would, you know, kill anyone."

"He's a dope dealer."

"Not a big one. Just to high school kids for parties, and it's mostly Percocet and Vicodin anyway. They're legal." He laughs. Not legal for recreational purposes, not to sell, especially not to minors. And I know this too.

He digs into his jeans pocket and brings out a twenty dollar bill. "You're gonna need this for Mexico."

"Wow." Now I laugh.

He shrugs. "It's all I got."

"Thanks Kev. I can use it." Taking the cash, I shift the Jetta into reverse. He steps back, then says, "Hey, Pep...I mean Nik. I'm sorry. About everything." The lopsided smile. The blue eyes. This is why my mother couldn't control me when I was seventeen. And why Holly stays.

I swerve onto the street with Kevin walking down the sidewalk after me, hands shoved in pockets. I smile. Can't help myself. We had good times. Like my mother on the phone to the cops, Kevin and me speeding away in his old Nissan Sentra with my granddad's '54 Stratocaster in my lap.

But I'm glad I'm not Holly. Grateful for Aunt Char, who gave me a place to stay. She wasn't exactly the kind of guardian Social Services would've found for me, but I got over Kevin and the loss of my baby by roaming the dusty hill next to the apartment, day and night, listening to Mary J, dancing in the clearing, and scrambling to the top of the Eagle Rock where all of LA spilled out at my feet like Legoland.

Then I met Tommy. Blissing out one afternoon after my shift at Tower Records, I ambled down the zigzag path that leads to the little park on Scholl Canyon Road. A tan Ford Explorer idled at the curb. I know now, but didn't know then, he'd just delivered drugs to some high school kids. They cruised up next to him before I'd come down the path, rolled down their passenger window, did the deal, and took off.

I was about to go back up to the Rock when Tommy climbed out and waved. I looked behind me because, of course, he didn't mean me, but he did.

"Hey you," he said with the emphasis on the "you." His smile was sexy, and for the first time since Kevin dumped me for Holly, I felt sexy too. We lasted a year. Then he met Chloe. And by that time, I knew I wanted out. So I was glad Chloe started hanging with us. Chloe flirting with Tommy, luring him away. Chloe who ended up on the cement steps with a hole in her neck. Not a walrus after all.

This is stupid, driving up Patrician Way toward the faded brown complex where I live to find out if anyone's found the body. Will the Rock be swarming with cops? There was nothing on TV at Kevin's. At least there hadn't been when I left. I'm not looking to give myself up, but I've got to know what's going on. Then I can decide what to do.

To my left, where the Rock looms at the top of the

hill, two cruisers block Eagle Vista Way. Beyond them more cars and a couple vans jam the area. I slow, scanning the front of my apartment building for Tommy's Explorer, and spy two cops lingering in the carport. In my carport? In my space? Waiting for *me?*

I wrench the steering wheel around and gun the engine back toward Colorado. Check my rearview. Can't see the cops. Where'd they go? Did they see me?

My heart thumps. My whole body thumps as I make the turn, sure that any second I'll hear a siren and see the flash of lights behind me.

I make it all the way to Eagle Rock Boulevard. No one after me. No one noticing me. Okay. Good.

My fingers are white on the steering wheel, my shoulders up at my ears, so I turn in at Walgreens and park. Breathe. Deep. Deep. Deeper. Exhale. I'm still trembling, but I force myself to climb out of the Jetta. Scan the lot for cops. I'll leave the car here. Walk to Grace's. She'll know if Tommy's involved, if the cops even know who Chloe's new boyfriend is. Was. What a mess.

But there's something else I have to do. My hair is long and curly with some awesome blond streaks, hair that people, especially guys, might remember. I use the twenty bucks Kevin gave me to buy a dark gray beanie, an extra-large man's T-shirt, cheap sunglasses, and some gloves, fingers missing, the kind men use for work.

As soon as I'm out of the store, shoulders stooped, head down, I duck into the Starbucks across the lot. I change in the restroom. The person in the mirror looks worried, but not much like me. With my hair hidden, I'm a skinny teen-age guy.

I stash my own clothes in the trash can and leave,

imitating Tommy's loping walk, right arm swaying as the right foot steps out. A wannabe rapper strut. And head for the apartment Grace shares with George.

Grace. I trust her. We're friends. Good friends now. At first, she hated me for stealing Tommy. Hated him almost as much. Then one Saturday night, a couple of weeks after Tommy and I'd gotten together, we headed to a DJ Klout concert in Riverside County, George driving. Tommy called shotgun, sending Grace grumbling to the back seat with me. I kept my sunglasses on and my head toward the window, not wanting her to notice me, muttering "no" when she shoved me the blunt.

When we stopped at a Snack Mart for beer, I went off on my own. Grace found me at the Oreos. "So?"

I moved away, not saying anything. She cut me off, turned her back to the cashier and stuffed a handful of Twix into her jeans. "What'd you say to Tommy?"

"What're you talking about?" I focused on the intricacies of unwrapping packaged snacks.

She grabbed one of my cookies and twisted it apart. Used her bottom teeth to scrape at the white insides.

"C'mon," she said. "What happened to your eye?"

"My eye?"

"Yeah. The one you're hiding behind those sunglasses. You walk into Tommy's fist?"

"No. I..."

"Don't shit me, Nik. Welcome to the club."

Grace lives in a rat hole in Highland Park with George because she doesn't have an Aunt Charlotte to leave her an apartment. I rap on the door, wondering if coming here is a big mistake. What if George answers, or Tommy, and they have something to do with Chloe's being dead? Maybe one of them put that gun in my hand so I'd take the blame.

I clench my fists. I'm not leaving.

When the door opens, I let go the breath I've been holding without knowing it.

"What do you want?" Grace frowns like she doesn't know me. I remember my "disguise" and take off the dark glasses. "Shit," she says, as she grabs my arm and steers me through the iron gate toward the side of the building.

"You gotta get out of here," she says. "The cops are looking for you." She nods at my outfit. "Guess you know about Chloe?"

I nod. The cops must've found my iPod. My cell. The gun. It never happens this fast on TV. "Are they here? In your apartment right now?"

Grace shivers, rubbing her hands up and down her arms as the warm afternoon sun disappears behind Mt. Washington. "No, but they were here earlier. Took all three of us to the station, but they let me go."

"Oh my God." I make myself smaller. Whisper, "How...how'd they know about us so fast?"

"Take a guess."

"*I* didn't call them." I say, thinking Holly. That bitch.

Grace peers at me hard. "Why would you call them?"

"I...didn't...wouldn't..." I almost lose it here, remembering Chloe on the steps. Me running away. "Oh, Grace, I saw her. She didn't have a neck."

Grace puts her hands on my shoulders, shakes me. "Okay. Calm down. Let me make sure the cops aren't spying on us. Then you can come in."

She slinks out the gate. Over her shoulder, she hisses, "Don't move."

Goosebumps break out under my T-shirt. I pace so I won't cry, kicking at the dandelions poking through the cracks in the cement, trying to get my brain straight. Thank God for Grace. I stare at the glow left by the sun and swear that if I get out of this, things will be different. I'm going back to community college, getting a real job. No more booze. No more drugs. No more slacker boyfriends. Nothing. Clean and sober.

I walk to the gate. Where is she? The street is filled with cars, too many apartments on this narrow street, but no one seems to be staking us out. I turn and lean against the gate, study a scraggly rose bush choked by weeds. Close my eyes. Count to ten. Screw this.

* * *

When I push inside Grace's gloomy apartment, the first thing she does is hand me a pipe. Grace and I bonded over drugs, but I don't want a hit. Instead I ask, "What were you doing? It's freezing out there."

"Making sure it was safe."

I strain to see through the darkness of the room. Something's different. No Coke cans litter the floor, no ashtrays spill over onto the battered coffee table. The usual pile of unfolded laundry is missing from the sofa.

"You clean up for me or the cops?" I joke. I don't know where to start, what to do.

"It's not that clean," says Grace, snatching the pipe. She leans back in the blue velour recliner, not looking at me, says, "I'm gonna split."

"What do you mean split? Go out and come back or leave forever?" I ask, thinking this last idea might be the right one. Grace and I always talk about leaving when we're kicking it on the broken steps under the Rock, smoking weed, and complaining about the guys and their slacker lives. Me more than Grace, but we keep putting it off. Waiting. For what? Something to happen.

Then Grace says, "George just called. They're being charged for dealing, and the cops are working on Tommy for murder. George wants you to go see that guy." She points at the coffee table. I pick up the *VIBE* magazine. Scribbled across Gwen Stefani's abs are the words *Spike and Sons Bail Bonds* and an address.

"They're actually arrested?"

"Yeah, but it's Tommy who's in real trouble."

"So you're taking off, just like that?"

"Tommy's getting what he deserves. He's a prick. I'm sick of him."

"What about George?"

"I've always been sick of George. Besides, I don't wanna be around in case the cops decide to pick me up again. I've already got a bus ticket."

I think about this. "Does George know you're leaving?"

"That's why he's asking you to run his errand."

"I can't," I say. "I don't have my car."

"Why not?"

"I left it at that drug store, the one by Starbucks. I figured if the cops were looking for me, they'd be looking for my car."

"That's pretty paranoid, Nik."

"Me? You're the one leaving town. When's your bus?

I could drop you at the station, and then take care of the bail."

She heads into the kitchen. Comes back with a large bag of Oreos. Bites into one. Chocolate crumbs dust her chin. "George needs my car."

"He has a car."

"Doesn't run. Look, Nik, let's not argue. The cops want to question you about Tommy and the drugs. It's no big deal. You can drive your own car."

I start to remind her that I saw the body, had the gun in my hand, when I realize I never finished telling her that I was the first one to find Chloe. And she hasn't asked. But it doesn't matter. The cops have Tommy. They might believe my story if I tell it straight. Take a lie detector test. Use Holly's cop friend to smooth the way. But I don't say any of this to Grace. Instead I ask, "Why do you think Tommy shot her?"

"God, Nik, you can be so brain-dead sometimes."

"Why? The worst thing he ever did to me was break my wrist and that wasn't his fault. I fell and it snapped."

"Nik. Nikki, listen to me, will you? *You* are not a narc. Chloe Moss is...was...a narc."

* * *

I can't believe it, but Grace should know. She'd been hauled down to the police station with George and heard all about it. So Chloe Moss, who looks—looked—18, turned out to be a 25-year-old undercover cop working Eagle Rock High School.

"I figure she was always on to Tommy," Grace says as she drives me back to my car.

"But they met by accident," I say. "He knocked her off her bar stool at the A & D Club. I was there." I'd been talking to Tommy's friends and glanced over just as he banged into her. They tussled a little. Playful. Laughing. Then he bought her a drink and they danced. When Tommy got back to the table, I was pissed. But he talked me out of it. As usual. Now that Grace brings it up, maybe Chloe made it happen. Maybe she moved purposefully into him, not him into her.

"I'm going back to Bakersfield to chill," says Grace as she pulls into the space next to my Jetta. "You'll be okay." She digs in her purse and pulls a business envelope. "Here's the money for George's bond. And Nik, forget about Tommy. None of us has enough money to help him, even if we wanted to."

I take the envelope and search her face. She has an angular jaw, thin lips. I'd grown used to them, but now they stand out, making her appear hard, bitter. She laughs at me. "Don't look so serious. George'll take care of you."

Nodding, I climb out and walk around to the driver's side of the Jetta. Grace waves. I don't wave back, but stare after her as she circles her way through the parking lot and out into the flow of traffic.

* * *

I don't go to the bail bondsman. Instead I make a quick phone call, and head up Colorado Boulevard, back through Eagle Rock, the town, toward Eagle Rock, the geological landmark. Perched on the hill above the 134 freeway, most of the Rock is shrouded in night, but a sliver of moon gleams on its southern face, illuminating the time-etched wings of the eagle.

When I turn onto Patrician Way, I flick off my headlights, but no cruisers block the cul-de-sac below the Rock. The street's deserted.

I park in a neighbor's empty stall in the apartment building carport and get out, quietly closing the door. I take in the street, scan the freeway, and finally turn toward the Rock. Adrenaline surges through the tops of my legs. My heart pounds. Every nerve in my body tingles. But I'm in a different place tonight. Without pills. Without even one suck on the pipe. No walrus can fool me now.

I move along the same ridge path I took last night. The weeds are trampled, the bits of trash gone. The cops have picked the hill clean.

My destination isn't the stairs, so when I get to the clearing, I angle across to the back side of the rock, where it's overgrown, jungle-like. Slowing, I make out the murmur of leaves and the *choop* of a shovel scooping dirt. My heart stops.

Ever since I realized Grace wasn't interested in the fact I'd seen Chloe's body last night, I've been trying to figure out why. Our lives aren't so depraved that the death of someone we know should be so...so...lacking in the need to discuss, dissect, analyze. It's what I'd gone to Grace's to do. But she didn't want any part of it.

As quietly as I can, I skirt the bottom of the rock and move into the bushes. Grace kneels on the ground, tugging something out of a hole, a shovel tossed carelessly at her feet. I suck in a breath.

Grace reels around. "What the hell are you doing here?"

"What the hell are *you* doing here?"

We glare at each other for one long moment. Then she pulls herself up, clutching something in her hand, and says calmly, "I was on the way to the bus station when I remembered this." She holds up a small metal cash box.

"What is that?" I ask, even though I know.

"Hey, why aren't you bailing George out?"

I step closer. Glance around. "I came back to see if I could find my cell phone or my iPod. I dropped them somewhere. You know, last night, when I was here."

"George is gonna be pissed."

"What's in the box, Grace?"

"Love letters. Some from George, some from Tommy. I'm sentimental, you know?"

"Really? Tommy never wrote me love letters."

"E-mails. Look, Nikki, I've got a bus to catch." She leans down, picks up her backpack, and starts sidling to her left toward the clearing.

I cut her off. She fumbles in her backpack. Drops it to the ground, and whips out a gun. Another gun? I hadn't thought about another gun. "Whoa," I say. "What're you doing?" I'm close enough to grab it, but I'm afraid to try. I move back.

"What I should've done back at my apartment. Dammit, Nikki, you don't have enough IQ to leave things alone, do you?"

The sight of the gun pointing at my chest makes me dizzy. I jam my nails into my palms to stay focused. "I'm just looking for my cell."

"Give it up," she says. "I know why you're here. You want the money and you can't have it. It's my money. I earned it."

"How'd you earn it, Grace, by killing Chloe? Are you

going to kill me too?"

"I have to. It was going to work out better the other way, but you screwed it up."

"You were here, Grace, weren't you, last night? The reason you didn't ask me about the body is you shot Chloe yourself. You put the gun in my hand."

"I wanted everything to be simple, but then you show up, dumb enough to pass out, and so I figured I'd twist you just like I was twisting Tommy."

"You knew Chloe was a narc?"

"Of course I did. That's why she and I met up here. I was going to be a snitch. At least that's what she thought, but I had a plan of my own."

"To kill Chloe and frame Tommy?"

"I don't want to talk about this anymore. Shut up and move back into the bushes."

My mouth goes dry, but I have to keep talking. Keep her talking. Stall. "Don't you want to know how I know?"

"I don't give a shit."

"You said none of us had enough money to help Tommy, but that isn't true."

"Move." Her voice is low, determined. I stumble toward where she's pointed the gun. She follows close behind.

My voice cracks when I say, "But Tommy has the money. If I knew about the cash box, you'd know. Is money worth killing for, Grace?"

"Money? Right, you don't get it. Tommy was the point. Getting Tommy. Now getting you." She pokes me hard with the gun. I think, NOW, and stop. She barrels into me, the gun knocking into my spine. I tumble forward, bringing her with me. Turn. Grab for the gun. She drops the cash box. Using both hands, she pulls the gun away, aims it straight at me just as I kick a high cheerleading kick, and nail her under her chin. She hits the ground, the gun bouncing into the weeds.

I lean over. Catch my breath. She crabs over for the gun, but I'm there, snatching it up, aiming it, and moving back. "Stay right there, Grace. I mean it."

"I think Miss Hyland does mean it." The firm male voice comes from somewhere behind me. Grace jerks around as two police officers emerge from the brush, guns drawn.

The shorter one nods at me, "Thank you, Nikki. We can take it from here. Holly Garcia sends her regards."

* * *

"Isabel, want some juice?" I ask. The little rug-rat holds on to my leg, finger in her mouth, staring up at me. Over the past few weeks, we've become best friends.

"Duice. Duice," she says. I pull out the orange juice, the one with a hand-labeled sign that says "Izzie and Nikki" on it and pour it into her sippy cup. She takes it in both hands and gulps it. Just like her dad. Only cuter.

"I'll be back," says Holly, as she breezes into the kitchen. She's wearing an aerobics outfit, cheeks glowing. She's training to be a fitness instructor. I'm baby-sitting.

"What time does your class start?" she asks.

"12:30. You've got plenty of time."

"What's the class?"

"ADMJ 110. The role and responsibilities of each segment within the administration of the justice system."

She laughs and gives me a thumbs-up. "Bet Tommy has a fit when he finds out."

"Tommy won't believe it. But by the time he gets out of jail, I'll be in uniform and packing, so no more fraternizing with known felons for me."

Holly laughs again and wraps her arms around Isabel. "Bye, baby girl. Mommy'll be back soon."

I guess we're growing up.

* * *

The sun is warm on my shoulders as I climb to the top of the Eagle Rock, the sky above an aquamarine bowl. Smiling, I plop down on the gritty surface.

I breathe in the sweet afternoon air and spread my arms like an eagle. Me, sitting on this damn Rock with the whole world at my feet. It's all good.

Arguably, the antithesis of downtown L.A.'s famous Biltmore Hotel would be the 1,470-room **Bonaventure Hotel**, *where old-world charm has given way to post-modern glitz. Built in 1976, the 35-story Bonaventure looks like a set piece straight out of a science-fiction thriller, with its five cylindrical, mirrored-glass towers, and glass elevators that shoot through the lobby roof to crawl up the hotel's shimmering exterior. In fact, Hollywood has used this dazzling landmark as a setting for dozens of movies including* **Blue Thunder** *and* **Rain Man**. *One of the ten most-photographed buildings in the world, the Bonaventure is also one of the most recognizable buildings in downtown L.A.'s skyline. Moreover, the high-tech design doesn't end with its exterior. Inside the cavernous hotel, you'll find a circular, soaring five-acre atrium that houses retail stores, restaurants and bars, an indoor "lake' and numerous fountains. Within this hub of human activity, your powers of observation will be tested, and sometimes, what you see is not always, what you get...*

JUST LIKE OLD TIMES
by G. B. Pool

After taking a week off, I still felt lousy. I had just renewed my P.I. license, worked four days; two people died, one a friend, but I solved the case. Sad consolation.

I headed back to my place in the mountains outside L.A. early Sunday evening and got my usual table at Rusty's Diner. A local band was onstage. Somebody said they played backup in a recording studio down in Hollywood for a couple of Country Western singers, but I didn't recognize their names. Where I came from in New Jersey, "country" meant Canada and "western" meant Pennsylvania.

After ordering a beer and bratwurst, I sat back and listened to the music. It was starting to grow on me. At least you could understand the words. How bad could a guy be who loved his dog, his truck, *and* his girl?

My cell phone rang. I was lucky to get service that far back in the woods. Logjam was just about as far off the beaten track as you could get without ending up in Barstow.

"Hello?"

"Johnny, is that you?" said Iris.

Iris Sherwood was a retired actress who rented my other house in Los Angeles. The place was a bit of a relic, just like she was. Iris was Old Hollywood. Very Old

Hollywood. She knew every actor who was anybody from the 30's through the 60's. Hedda Hopper would have hocked her hats for the scoops she could have gotten from the venerable star. But Iris, in her mid-eighties, knew how to keep secrets. And bless her heart, the old gal was a character herself, and that had nothing to do with the ones she played on the silver screen.

"You called me, Iris. What is it?"

"Oh, good, he's there," she said to someone with her on the other end of the phone. "Johnny, I need you."

"Is something wrong?" Two weeks earlier she really had a problem, so I couldn't say she always cried wolf.

"Nothing's wrong, silly. I want you to come for dinner tomorrow. Please say yes, Johnny, dear. It's time I did something nice for you."

"Dinner. Uh…I'm kinda tired, Iris."

"Tired! How can a young man like you be tired? I'm twice your age and never had a tired day in my life. Now, what do you say? Eight o'clock tomorrow. Okay?"

What the hell, I thought. Another change of scenery might be just what the doctor ordered. "Sure, Iris. Eight o'clock."

"We will be dressing for dinner, Johnny. Black tie," she added before hanging up.

I put down my cell phone and said out loud, "What did she expect me to do, come in my bathrobe?"

"Going someplace, Johnny?" said a voice to my right.

I turned to see Logjam's resident mortician. He wasn't the tall, gaunt, gray man from the Boris Karloff movies. Harold Kane was shorter, plumper, and pinker.

"I've been invited to dinner. The lady told me 'black tie.' Please tell me, in laid-back California terms, that doesn't mean tuxedo."

"Sorry, Johnny. I'd loan you one of ours, but they all button up the back. The Bridal Boutique next to Abigail's Flowers rents them."

"I thought I could get through my entire life without having to wear one of those get-ups. I wonder if I still have a tie."

"A bow tie," he clarified.

"Bow tie?"

"And opera slippers," he added.

"I'm not wearing slippers. I'll starve first."

"You're going to a formal dinner?" he questioned.

"Yeah. I guess. Can't I wear plain shoes to a fancy dinner?"

"They'll have to be patent leather."

"I'll be a customer of yours before I wear patent leather shoes, Harold."

"It's traditional."

"Are you telling me the guys wearing tuxedoes in the movies are wearing ballet shoes?"

"Opera slippers. And yes, probably."

"Oh, for crying out loud. James Bond? Bogart wore 'em?" He nodded. "No wonder they were tough guys. You'd have to be if you were wearing ballet slippers."

I spent my youth holed up in cheap hotel rooms watching old movies hour after hour on a thirteen-inch black and white TV set fitted with a pair of rabbit ears, waiting for sleazy little guys to bring me the take from the numbers operation I ran in Jersey for Big Louie Bonnano, and then later when I ran a floating bookie joint down in Miami for Big Eddie Fontaine. And here I thought George Raft was so tough.

The next day I bought myself a new tuxedo and dress shoes. Not patent leather and not slippers, just plain black shoes. I had the clerk show me how to tie the frigging bow tie and how to strap on the cummerbund. All I kept thinking was, this better be a damn good dinner, Iris.

The drive down the mountain into Los Angeles took two and a half hours. There wasn't much traffic coming from that direction, but it's still a long haul from my place on the lake to the Petit Palace, as Iris called it, just off Los Feliz Boulevard. The five thousand square foot California villa was left to me in the will of a grateful client. All that gold trim and the painted ceilings and the Louis Something furniture was too much for an old boy from the rough side of Jersey City. The only painted ceilings I ever saw were done with a spray can.

If there is the reverse of claustrophobia, that house gave it to me. The joint had seven bathrooms and I'm pretty sure I never saw more than three of them. That's why I hired a real estate firm to rent it for me and I moved up here to yokeldom, where I rattle around in twenty-five hundred square feet of knotty pine. But with all the trees and ducks and bears and tourists, it still gives me that crowded, urban feeling.

I pulled into the villa's circular drive in my SUV. I wasn't alone. I must have missed the part when Iris said she was having other guests. I knew Parker would be there. Chalkie Parker was Iris's manservant, her former lover, and her constant companion. Parker was also a world-class jewel thief who hung up his burglar tools before I was born. Yeah. Iris was good at keeping secrets.

By the look of the vehicles in the driveway, the last of Old Hollywood was dining with us. Three of the cars came with drivers decked out in black suits and cloth caps. They stood beside their vehicles polishing the antique paint. When I ran the bookie joint for Big Eddie, I'd take some of these beauties for collateral when my customers couldn't pay up. Sometimes Big Eddie would just take them…period.

The first car was a 1937 Cord Convertible, snow white, with its leather top down. Next to it was a black 1934 Ford Sedan. It looked like one of those cars Edward G. Robinson drove in his gangster movies. There was a pink Cadillac convertible, too. The 1959 Eldorado Biarritz with a set of fins that could swim to Catalina. And sitting all by itself under the arbor was a cherry-red Corvette, the 1958 model with white walls and chrome trim.

I love my SUV, but, oh, baby. My mouth was open and I was in serious jeopardy of stepping on my tongue.

"Careful, son. They're addictive."

Chalkie Parker was standing in the doorway smiling at me. He was still wearing those white gloves and I think I figured out why. Fingerprints. His former occupation had him wanted on three continents.

"Don't tell me," I said. "Old fans are sending Iris tokens of their appreciation."

"And don't think she didn't get a few automobiles, my smart friend. But, alas, no. These belong to our…Iris's other guests." He noticed my duds. "You clean up good, Mr. Casino. A regular Cary Grant." He looked at my street shoes and smiled.

Just a few weeks earlier I had been sitting in the same house, having a quiet whiskey in the library with Parker. This night the villa had been transformed. It was the first time I really thought of the place as a palace. The crystal chandeliers sparkled brighter than a king's ransom.

The walls glowed and it had nothing to do with the paint. The reason stood under the Italian chandelier in the foyer.

Iris. Wearing a vintage lace gown with a high collar from one of her prehistoric movies, she was more radiant than the strands of pearls around her wizened neck. Her thinning hair was piled on her head like a queen's, and true to her style, she wore a tiara. Knowing Iris, those were real stones.

"Johnny! My hero!" She put her frail arm around my neck and pulled me close to her. Softly, she gave me a little kiss.

"Iris, I didn't do anything," I tried to say.

"Not the diamond caper," she whispered. "You're all over television. Private detective Johnny Casino saves congressman. I've been getting calls all week wanting to know when you'd be back in town and back in business."

"I'm not moving to Los Angeles, Iris. I'm gonna work out of Logjam."

"Logjam! Why? The action is here in L.A., big guy."

I heaved a sigh and hoped she'd go on to other things.

"Come and meet my other guests," she said. "They're dying to meet you. Oh, maybe at their ages, I shouldn't say 'dying.'" She winked and dragged me into the living room.

"My dears, may I present Johnny Casino, Private Eye."

I was instantly transported into the first reel of one of those film noirs I used to watch, except this one was in living color. I recognized the faces, even though they were several decades older in this version.

Jack Davis was the oldest actor there. He was doing tough-guy movies with Cagney when he was nineteen and love scenes with Crawford when he was twenty. His first acting job was in a crowd scene in a 1928 silent picture with Greta Garbo. He told Iris that Garbo talked more in the movie than she did on the set.

As for Jack, he loved to talk about every movie ever made. At 92, his memory was still as sharp as his attire. His suit looked like he had borrowed it from William Powell.

Vera Hollcroft was the kid in the group, only 85. She made a career playing the gun moll in those 1940's flicks. Her memory was failing, and half the time you'd think she was doing a scene from *Sunset Boulevard*, except Vera really thought DeMille would be calling her for that close-up.

Howard Anderson was the quiet one. He was blessed with a head of snow-white hair and was usually cast as the wise old family doctor. More than once he would slowly turn toward the other characters in the scene with him, shake that stately mane and solemnly pronounce, "I'm sorry. He's dead."

Rupert Campbell was wearing a charcoal gray pinstriped suit. He must have come in the Ford. He looked like a gangster. His hair had thinned to eight or ten strands that were now plastered over the top of his head along with a handful of liver spots, but he still had a commanding look.

Rupe spent his entire career doing Mafioso types, yet when he read for Brando's part in *The Godfather*, the producers said he didn't look Italian. His claim to fame was that he died in every movie he ever made. He'd recreate his death scene at the drop of a hat, even at the ripe old age of 90. He couldn't fall onto the carpet anymore, but he would slump into a chair and do the scene from a sitting position.

After the introductions, we ate. I didn't know people really lived like that. Imported caviar. French Champagne.

Even the lobsters flew in from Maine. I wonder how they got through security?

For dessert Parker wheeled in a trolley with something fully engulfed in flame. I jumped out of my chair and was going to hit it with a pitcher of water before Iris calmed me down and told me it was supposed to be on fire. She called it Cherries Jubilee.

After five courses, we found ourselves sitting in the library enjoying after-dinner drinks. The liquor was good. Most of the geriatric crowd sipped theirs. As for me, I was trying hard to keep up with Rupert, who could have drunk Richard Burton under the table. I had trained my palate to love 12-year old Scotch. I had no idea how good the 18-year old variety was. I do now. I was on my third shot when we settled in for what I figured would be an all-night gab session. Most of the movie stars the old fossils talked about during dinner had long since faded from the scene, but the stories were great.

"Clark was married to Joan at the time," said Vera. "I heard her tell the story to Natalie Moorhead."

"Gable was never married to Crawford," interrupted Howard. "But they did spend more time together making pictures than he did with his first wife. And you know Clark. He had gotten used to the good life by then. He was married to Rhea at that point. Joan was just another hoofer."

Iris shook her head. "No, no, no. Joan was out of the chorus line by 1928. She was a leading lady before Clark got his first speaking part."

"That's right," confirmed Jack. "It was 1931. Clark and Joan did three pictures that year. He did only one with Norma, *A Free Soul*."

"And from what I heard," said Vera, in what sounded like a stage whisper, "Adela Rogers St. Johns wrote that one especially for Joan, and Norma, that cat, told Irving Thalberg she wanted it, or else."

"And whatever Norma wanted, Norma got," said Iris.

"She didn't get the Scarlett O'Hara part," said Jack.

"And you know why," said Iris, assuming everyone knew the story.

"She didn't like Clark Gable's wooden teeth," said Vera, getting her stories confused.

"Those were George Washington's wooden teeth," said Jack, correcting her.

That further befuddled Vera. "Clark Cable borrowed George Washington's teeth?"

Everyone took a healthy swallow of his or her drink. Everyone except Vera, who was still contemplating Clark Gable at Valley Forge.

I drank down the last of my Scotch and stood up to pour myself another drink. Parker might have been the butler during these soirees, but he was nodding off in a tall, wingback chair, not terribly interested in hearing stories he had listened to for fifty years. That's when I heard it. Parker's eyes twitched and he sat up. We were both looking at the library door when two armed men ran into the room.

"Hands up! All of you."

One man was my age, early forties, but he looked like he'd done hard time. Maybe it was the sallow complexion that said he'd spent three to five as a guest of the State. And his baggy clothes belonged to someone two sizes larger. The other guy was mid-thirties, and his clothes fit better.

Parker stepped forward.

"Don't move, pops," said the older thug.

I glanced at Parker. He squeezed his elbow against his side like he was feeling for a shoulder holster and then looked at me. I shook my head slightly. He shrugged. I never go anywhere without packing heat except for that night, wearing that stupid monkey suit. I made a mental note to myself, to never, ever, leave home without a weapon again.

Not all of us in the room with the gunmen realized the gravity of the situation. Vera spoke first.

"Iris! Entertainment. How wonderful. This is a lot better than your last party, dear. But what does his costume represent?"

"She's right, Iris," said Howard. "He needs to borrow one of Jack's old pinstripes. Hey, Jack. You got one to fit this mug?"

"I'm not here for laughs, old man," said the guy. "Which one of you is Johnny Casino?"

All eyes turned in my direction. "I'm Johnny Casino. What can I do for you?"

"I need your help."

"Excuse me?"

He lowered his gun a fraction and I saw a plaintive look on his face. "You're supposed to be smart. I heard about you on TV."

"This isn't exactly the place to talk business," I said. "Let's leave here and—"

"No!" barked the other guy, waving his revolver. "We stay here. These old folks are our hostages."

"*Hostages?*" questioned Vera. "What does he mean hostages? Have we been kidnapped?"

"It's okay, Vera," said Jack. "This punk won't be here long."

"Whadda ya mean, punk?" said the punk. "I've been in jail."

"And you'll be doing a return engagement quite shortly," said Jack.

"Why you old—"

"Shut up, Beans," said the brains of the outfit.

"If you want me," I said, "you'll have to let these folks go."

"That's not the way it's going down, Casino," said the leader. "They're my leverage. Get rid of the kitchen help. No funny business or somebody will get hurt. Beans, you go with him."

"Sure, Mike. Come on, Casino."

With Beans standing just outside the kitchen door, jabbing me in the back with his gun, I managed to dismiss the caterer and her staff with a hurried explanation and a handful of bills.

Returning to the library, I was faced with wide eyes and worried looks.

"What do you want?" I asked this Mike character.

"Beans, you watch these old people while I take Casino here for a little ride. And Beans, do...not...hurt... them..in...any...way."

He gave his instructions like he was writing them on a chalkboard in large block letters. Beans let the words sink in like a dog learning a new trick.

"Okay, okay, boss. You be back soon?"

"When I'm through with Casino."

"Don't you dare hurt him," said Iris, standing up to the hoodlum.

"Don't worry, lady," said Mike. "He's only in trouble if he doesn't help me."

Mike motioned me to leave. I gave a slight shrug to Parker and headed through the foyer and out the front door. We walked past the chauffeurs, down the driveway, and finally to a beat-up Chevy parked three blocks away.

"Just tell me what this is all about," I pleaded. "I don't want Beans to do anything to those old folks."

"He won't hurt 'em. His gun isn't even loaded." I started to move toward him. "Mine, on the other hand, is. But I'll tell you this, Mr. Casino, I have no intention of hurting you. I need your help."

"You have a strange way of asking for it. What kind of trouble are you in?"

"I want you to solve a murder."

"Is that why you were in jail?"

"I see you recognized my jailhouse tan. But, I was in for robbery, not murder."

"Who do they think you killed?"

"I don't know," he said.

"I don't get it. Why do you think they'll blame you?"

"Get in the car and I'll tell you."

I opened the passenger door and started to get in. I could see another man in the seat.

"Excuse me," I said. The man didn't answer. "Uh, do you want me to get in the back?" Silence. I stood up and asked Mike, "What am I supposed to do here?"

"Find out who this guy is..." With a slight touch of Mike's hand, the stiff fell forward. "And who killed him."

"If it were me, I'd push him off a cliff and let somebody else find him. Why don't you just go to the police?"

"With my record? I'm not supposed to associate with felons. Just think what the cops would do if I turned up with this guy."

"You associate with Beans."

"I don't know anybody else dumb enough to pull a stunt like this, Mr. Casino."

"Call me Johnny."

"My name is Mike Levine. I am...or was, a bank robber by trade."

"Your friend, Beans, is in that house scaring the hell out of those people. Let's do our talking back there."

"You'll help me?"

"You have any money?"

"Where's the nearest bank?"

We both grinned.

We went back to the house. The scene had changed slightly since our departure. The seniors were sitting at a table playing cards. Beans was tied up on the floor.

"That didn't take long," said Parker.

"I was going to say the same thing. How did you...?" I indicated the trussed up punk.

"Iris hit him over the head with a silver tray and I hit him with a Louis Fifteenth chair. I hated to do it. It was a lovely chair. Johnny, his gun wasn't even loaded. What's this all about?"

"I think Mr. Levine is about to tell us," I said to Parker. "Pour us another drink and we'll straighten this out."

Somebody suggested we untie Beans. He's lucky we didn't take a vote because he would have lost. Soon afterward we got down to business.

"Who has it in for you?" I asked Mike.

He didn't hesitate. "Vincent Merrick. I used to work for him."

"What does he do?" I asked.

"Owns a bank."

"Did you rob it?"

"This man's a kidnapper *and* a bank robber!" exclaimed Vera.

"We're not kidnapped anymore, dear," said Iris.

"I robbed banks when Merrick needed a cash infusion," said Mike. "I never hit his place."

"Why would he dump the dead guy on you?"

"What dead guy?" asked Rupert.

"Is this the plot to a new movie?" asked Vera.

"Hush," said Iris.

"As soon as I got out of jail he wanted me back working for him," explained Mike. "Look, Johnny, I've got a girl now. I want to go straight. He won't let me."

"Does he have anything on you…except the stiff in the car?"

"Yeah. I finger him and he tells the cops about all the other jobs I pulled. I'll do twenty years."

"You must have been pretty good," I said.

"He couldn't be that good," said Rupert. "He got caught."

"I let myself get caught," said Mike. "I wanted out."

"Why would a banker have you rob other banks?" I asked.

"He needed money. He lives large, and frankly, he has a mean streak."

"How many banks did you have to knock over to keep him happy?" asked Howard.

"None were big takes. Four, five hundred thousand a job. I'd do three, four heists a year."

"Were the other bankers in on it?" I asked.

"No. But he knew who would be making large

deposits."

"That was convenient," said Howard.

"Nothing convenient about it," said Mike.

"That reminds me of a picture Rupe and I did back in '42," said Jack. *"Death Comes Knocking.* Rupe's character was knee-deep in debt. He forces me to rob him so he can collect the insurance money."

"Yeah. But I get mine in the end," said Rupert. "I had a great death scene in that picture. Five lines." He paused to recall his exact dialogue. Getting into character, he said, "Is dis how you pay me back? With a bullet. I pulled you outta da gutter. I made you. You were nothin' without Big Frankie. You'll be nothin' again. Nothin', ya see. I made you." He coughed twice.

Rupert dropped his head onto the card table and theatrically expired. We all watched in rapt amazement. Mike looked at Rupert, and then looked at me.

"I think Vince Merrick blackmails his accomplices, too."

"Blackmail!" said Iris. "The swine."

"How does he get them to go along with him?" I asked.

"He must have somebody on the inside telling him who's vulnerable," Mike said.

"You did three, four robberies a year?" I asked. He nodded. "It would be hard to plant an accomplice inside each business with that much success. What did these suckers have in common?"

"Most of them had businesses in the Bonaventure Hotel," said Mike. "That's where Merrick's bank is."

"That sounds more like a bug infestation," I said.

"What are you talking about, Johnny?" asked Jack. "A

cockroach with a tape recorder?"

"Not quite, Mr. Davis," I said. "You can bug an office with something no bigger than a breath mint nowadays."

"Can I say something?" asked Beans, who had been sitting quietly on the sofa.

"Make it short," said Mike.

"Why don't we dump the stiff back in Mr. Merrick's lap? I never liked him anyway."

The group looked at each other and then at Beans. We had to admit, the idiot had a good idea.

"Hmm," I said, pondering the punk's suggestion. "Maybe we can kill two birds with one stone. Mike, has Merrick told you who the next victim is?"

"Yeah. We were gonna use a guy we hit the year before I got busted, but Merrick changed his mind. Now it's an import/export guy."

"Why did he change victims?" I asked.

"I really don't know. It's the first time one of his marks backed out. But I'm not in on the set up. Merrick does all the arm twisting himself."

"What was the other guy's name?" I asked.

"Armand Boussac."

Iris gasped.

"You know him?" I asked her.

"I buy some of my jewelry from Armand. He serves such wonderful teacakes in his delightful little shop."

I had a thought. "Iris, what does Armand look like?"

"Fernando Lamas. Only shorter."

I looked over at Mike. "That pretty well describes the stiff in your car, doesn't it, Mike?"

"Sure does."

"That explains the change of plans," said Rupert.

"Okay, Johnny, what do we do next?"

I looked at Rupert and then noticed all the old fools were smiling at me. "I work alone, folks." They kept smiling. "Really. This could get dangerous."

"This reminds me of a picture I saw in '65," said Jack. *"The Game Never Ends.* It was one of those new-fangled anti-hero plots where everybody was a thief, but the movie had this clever twist..."

Jack explained the film. I could tell before he got to the final credits he had outlined a winning plan. My only hope was that Vincent Merrick never saw the movie.

It took twenty-four hours to plot our strategy.

The first thing Wednesday morning Iris & entourage arrived at the front desk of the Bonaventure. Parker had called ahead for reservations and asked the hotel manager to arrange assistance for two invalid women who would be arriving in wheelchairs, one being famed screen actress Iris Sherwood. The group, including "Doctor" Howard Anderson, was escorted to two of the glass elevators and then to a suite of rooms on one of the upper floors. It was an expensive suite, so the help was lavish.

At about the same time, Jack Davis's driver drove up to the entrance in the '37 Cord and helped the old man out of the car and into a small, collapsible wheelchair that he pulled from the trunk. Jack wheeled himself into the lobby and made his way to the Bistro, where he sat and ordered coffee and crullers. He had positioned his chair as close to the entrance of Merrick's bank as he could before he placed what looked like a radio on the table and adjusted a generic walkman headset over his ears. He sat there tapping his fingers to imaginary music.

Mike went to Merrick's bank before they opened for

business, and said he would go along with the heist, but he said he wanted a bigger cut. One greedy guy understands another. The deal was set. As Mike left Merrick's office, he placed a small listening device under the desk. I had done a little shopping the day before and secured a few electronic toys. I was surprised how sophisticated the gadgets had become while I was retired.

Now it was my turn. I parked a rented van with a hydraulic lift tailgate in an outside lot and walked to the hotel. I wasn't alone. In a wheelchair scrubbed of any fingerprints was poor Mr. Boussac, covered with a blanket around his shoulders and over his lap and a hat pulled low over his face.

I was dressed like an orderly, with white cotton gloves. I continually bent over my charge taking silent orders from a very demanding corpse.

"Yes, Mr. Jones. I'll get you a nice cup of tea. What?... Of course. Would you like your usual table?...Yes, sir. Right away."

We picked an ordinary name for our unwanted guest and hoped for the best. The plan was that no one would recognize Boussac if we had him bundled up like a beggar.

On cue I rolled him up to Jack's table.

"Why, Fred. You old scoundrel," Jack said to the dead guy.

I reached under the blanket and managed to lift Boussac's arm just enough so Jack could grab the hand and shake it. At just that moment the waitress sidled up.

"Hello, Monsieur Boussac. Your usual?" she said.

Oh, Christ, I thought. I shoulda wrapped Boussac up in bandages before dragging him out in public. One yelp out of the waitress when she sizes up the stiff, and the entire

Over-The-Hill gang will be sharing digs at San Quentin. Fortunately, my Thespian friend knew what to do when an actor forgets his lines.

Jack turned his back to the woman and in a low tone ad-libbed a very raspy, *"Oui."*

I leaned over the dead man and began patting him on the back, emitting small coughs as I did. "You stay wrapped up, sir. *Cough, cough.* No need spreading that flu bug to everybody."

The waitress backed away as Jack continued, "Bring me another cup of coffee, my dear. And my friend's usual."

"Yes, sir." She scooted off.

"Now what?" asked Jack, panicked that Boussac's cover was blown.

"We play it by ear. Speaking of ear, have you overheard anything?"

"Merrick's a full-fledged pig. He called the import-export guy on his speakerphone the minute Mike left and told him to get down to his office on the double."

At that moment, the glass elevator behind us descended. A short Chinese man made a beeline to Merrick's bank.

"That must be him," said Jack. "He sounded like Charlie Chan."

The bank still wasn't open, but a small staff was getting ready for the business day to begin. A tall woman in a skin-tight suit that said she was more into pleasure than business unlocked the door and let the nervous man enter. His eyes dropped to the ground when he saw her. She jerked her head in the direction of Merrick's office. He slunk into the room. I grabbed the earphones and listened.

"I cannot do this, Mr. Merrick," said a heavily

accented voice. "It not good."

"I can ruin you with one phone call, Mr. Chang. Anyway, what have you got to lose? Your bank's insured."

"But—"

"Did you tell your buyer you had to be paid in cash?"

"Yes. I tell him my offshore investment company trade only in cash. He understand."

"I just bet he did. You two be at Taipei Bank at exactly ten o'clock tomorrow. It shouldn't take more than thirty minutes to make the transfer and get that money in the bank manager's hot little hands. The minute we see you step out of his office with the receipt, we'll make our move."

"What you promise me. When do I get it?" asked Chang.

"It'll be delivered by courier before you get back to your shop."

"But no more, Mr. Merrick," said Chang. "No more."

If that was a threat, it was a lousy one. Mr. Chang left Merrick's office, his head still down as he shuffled out of the bank. I heard Merrick's secretary walk into his office, but I wanted to follow Chang instead of listening. I handed the earphones back to Jack and sprinted after the man. We rode the elevator to the fifth floor and got out.

I didn't know what to make of this guy. It sounded like he was in on the heist after all and I wanted to get the goods on him. He slowly unlocked his shop door and went in, locking it behind him. He sat behind a hand-carved teakwood desk and bowed his head. Finally he dropped his head into his hands.

"Hum," I said to myself.

I got on one of the three glass elevators in that sector. Another elevator stopped on the same floor within eyeshot.

I watched through the glass as a man jerked his head to tell his woman to get on board. When she didn't move fast enough, he grabbed her arm and shoved her inside. Her eyes dropped to the floor in submission as they rode out of sight. It was the same submissive expression Chang had on his face when Merrick's secretary was brow beating him earlier.

I opened my cell phone and called Parker. "I know how Merrick gets his victims." I explained my theory and told him what to do.

The first thing I noticed when I got to the lobby was that our dear, departed friend had departed.

"Where's Boussac?" I asked.

"Rupert thought he should get him out of the way since the waitress recognized him. He took him up to the suite."

"We need him down here before Iris makes her move."

"I'll ring his room," said Jack.

"Anything going on in the bank?" I asked.

"Lots of heavy breathing in Merrick's office."

"The secretary's still in there?"

"Some secretary."

"Yeah. I think the lady is our common denominator."

At just that moment, the woman came out of Merrick's office. She headed for the teller windows while fastening the top button of her blouse and fixing her lipstick. That's when Merrick's phone rang.

"This should be it," I said. "Tell Rupert to return Boussac."

Merrick wasn't using the speakerphone this time, but I didn't need to hear the other side of the conversation. I knew what the dapper man on the other end was asking. His employer had a small fortune in jewels that needed safekeeping for two or three days while she was staying in town. She refused to let the hotel take charge of them because she had seen too many movies about famous women having their jewels stolen in these fancy hotels.

Merrick asked the name of this grande dame. He actually knew Iris Sherwood's name and reputation. Iris will be happy she wasn't forgotten.

"I'll be more than glad to keep Miss Sherwood's jewels in my safe. Can you give me an estimate of their value? I'll probably have to add extra security. No additional cost to you, of course."

I could just imagine Merrick's reaction when Parker rattled off the seven-figure sum in his greedy little ear.

"I'll make all the arrangements, Mr. Parker. I'll call you back in one hour so we can make sure the transfer is secure."

No sooner did he hang up than he dialed another number. I knew his next call would be to Mike Levine.

I turned to update Jack, but he was still on his cell phone. I mouthed the name: Rupert? He shook his head. He mouthed: Iris. I shrugged and mouthed: What? He handed me the phone.

"What is it, Iris?"

"It's Vera. You better come."

I rode the space age elevator through the glass ceiling in the hotel's atrium and found myself clinging to the side of that ultramodern edifice. The elevator pod was now on the exterior of the building. On the 28th floor, Howard was at their door hurrying me along.

"What is it?" I asked.

"Stage fright," said Howard.

"Pay attention, Vera," Iris was saying. "It's very

simple. You want to close your account. You wheel yourself up to the teller and say your lines."

Vera was getting frustrated. She tried to get into character. "But, Iris, I don't have an account at that bank."

"I know, dear, but they don't. Now you have to get this right. Try it again."

Vera wheeled her chair around and faced Iris who was standing behind the bar in the hotel room. She took a deep breath and said, "I'm here to rob the bank."

"No, Vera," said Iris. "You don't want to rob it. You want to close your account. Try again."

"How long has this been going on?" I asked Howard.

"Since we got here. She has that line in her head and we can't shake it loose."

"Vera," I said, turning her around and looking into her eyes. "This is a major role. You must believe that you have money in that bank. You feel it here." I patted my chest. "Now we'll go downstairs and you make them believe it. Are you ready?" I framed her face like framing a camera angle and slowly backed away. "Action."

Parker pushed Iris. Howard had Vera. And I took Mr. Boussac. We rode separate elevators. I looked at my watch. Right on time.

Iris and Parker were the first customers of the day. Merrick was on them like a rash.

"You're early," he said. "I haven't finished making the arrangements." He couldn't keep his eyes off the two large jewelry boxes on Iris's lap. "Wait in my office." He ushered them partway through the security door, the exact time Vera and "Doctor" Anderson made their entrance. Vera's voice echoed through the ultra modern bank.

"Service! Service, please," she said.

Merrick snapped his fingers and one of the tellers waved her over. Howard hobbled across the floor, giving me time to push Boussac near the deposit slip counter in the center of the room. I pulled out a form and started writing on it, holding my breath until Vera spoke. Meanwhile Parker managed to stick a small magnetic device across the electronic latch going to the office and vault areas.

Vera eased herself to the edge of her wheelchair and looked the teller in the eye. I saw her chest rise as she inhaled deeply and then said in a very clear voice. "I'm here to...close my account."

Breathing again, I watched as Vera continued her scene. In less than forty-five seconds it was discovered that she had no account at the bank.

"Thieves!" yelled Vera. "Thieves!" she yelled again.

Iris and Parker were just getting settled in Merrick's office. Vera's outburst brought him running. While Merrick was putting out that fire, Jack rolled into the bank in his wheelchair and positioned himself directly behind me. If I got the placement right, the surveillance cameras would see him enter, but they couldn't see him sitting behind me from any angle.

I looked at the clock. Zero hour.

Mike stormed in wearing a ski mask and waving a gun. "This is a holdup!" He pushed the front doors shut and flipped the CLOSED sign into view. "Everybody into the back. Move it!"

A teller released the catch on the security door so we could enter the rear. Wheelchairs were rolled into the safe deposit area. It was Vera and Howard, Boussac and me, two tellers, the sexy secretary, Merrick, and Mike. Funny, only the tellers looked nervous, really nervous. As for Jack, he was kneeling behind the center counter. I had hooked his folded wheelchair on the back of Boussac's chair under the blanket.

Mike pointed to Merrick. "You. In the vault."

Merrick led the way. In the hallway he whispered, "You're half an hour early. I haven't got the jewels yet."

Mike tapped his watch. "It's broken."

"Steal a new one," growled Merrick. Then pointing to his office, he added, "They're in there. Take the two cases and leave."

Before Mike could push Merrick into the office, Iris wheeled herself into the hallway. Mike spotted the jewel cases.

"My lucky day. I'll take those, lady."

Mike grabbed the boxes and was turning to leave when he ran smack dab into Rupert who had used the electronic release I provided to unlatch the security door after entering the bank.

"Excuse me," said Rupert. "The doors were closed during business hours. Hey, what's—"

"Out of my way, old man," said Mike.

"Why you young—"

A shot rang out. Rupe grabbed his chest and then slumped on the counter. "I knew there was trouble," he said. "I only wanted to help." He coughed twice before sinking slowly to the floor.

Mike dropped the jewel cases and fled. "Doctor" Howard stepped out of the safe deposit room and spotted the man on the floor. He knelt beside him and felt for a pulse. Then, looking up, he said solemnly, "I'm sorry. He's dead."

Iris yelled, "My jewels! My jewels!"

I was right behind Howard. I retrieved the cases and

handed them to her. "What's this?" I picked up a small tape recorder. "The robber must have dropped it."

I ran it back until it stopped and then hit the play button. We all heard Merrick's voice tell Mike to rob Iris.

"It looks like you're in deep trouble, Mr. Merrick," said Howard. "Someone call the police."

"I'll do it," said the secretary.

"I'll go with you," I said, "You, too, Merrick."

I followed them to the front. She started dialing a long number. I took the phone out of her hand and dialed a shorter one: 911.

Now it was Iris's turn. She raced her wheelchair from the hallway into the main room. "I want to go home. I knew I'd get robbed if I went out. Home, Parker."

Parker came up behind her and pushed the wheelchair across the room. Vera got her chariot into high gear with Howard chugging to keep up.

"Watch Merrick," I said to Parker.

I went back for Boussac and wheeled him into Merrick's office. I pulled the blanket from around his shoulders and retrieved the one on his lap as well as the hat. I opened the smaller wheelchair and popped it into position.

I could see Parker had done his job while in the office alone. Mike thought Merrick was blackmailing his victims. The leggy distraction in the tight suit looked like my idea of a high-priced leisure activity. I told Parker to search for pictures. The wall safe was open and a stack of videotapes was on the desk. Moving pictures would cost a target even more. I grabbed the one with Boussac's name on it and tucked it next to him. I stuffed another one into the pocket of my white coat before pushing the smaller wheelchair into the main bank area, having picked up a passenger along the way. Rupert, back from the dead, wrapped the blankets around himself as I pushed him into view.

It was a three-ring circus in there. Wheelchairs were rolling as the sound of sirens filled the air.

The cops cuffed Merrick on Iris's say-so. Who's to argue with a legend? The secretary wouldn't get far, once the District Attorney ran the videotape of her seducing the late Mr. Boussac.

A while later, I rode the elevator one more time. I'd done it so often I was getting the bends.

I went to Mr. Chang's shop. It was still locked. I knocked and waved the videocassette at him. With a questioning look on his face, he slowly approached and then unlocked the door.

"I believe this is yours," I said.

Jack was waiting for me when I got on the elevator to go back down. He said, "Johnny, this isn't the way that movie ended. The s.o.b. did it alone."

I looked out the glass capsule at my splendid cast of characters waiting below. "Life isn't a movie."

*No tour of L.A. Landmarks would be complete without a stop at the **Beach**, and L.A. boasts some of the best. Follow the scattered footprints along Will Rogers State Beach. Looking south, you can see the Ferris wheel at Santa Monica Pier turning lazily against the blue sky. Surfers wait for that perfect swell, and families spread out their picnics. Lovers camp under umbrellas and tourists burn red from the rays. In this sun-worshipper's paradise, everyone has a story to tell. Not every one has a happy ending. L.A.'s white sand beaches, with their palm trees and cool breezes lure the rich and famous. The down and out find their way here, too. Daily they arrive, lost souls seeking a better life, firm in their faith that their world can only get better at the beach. Maybe that's true...but what's that you see? A touch of evil drifting in on the tide...?*

MAKING IT WITH GAMMY
by Darrell James

Waiting for the man wasn't all that bad, Fremont decided. Sitting on a concrete wheel chock in the parking lot of the Will Rogers State Beach, he could look out on the ocean, smell salt air. Down the coast he could see the Santa Monica Pier, the Ferris wheel standing against the far-off backdrop of the Palos Verdes cliffs, and all of Malibu the other way, man. Majestic.

A bike path ran parallel to the beach, right on the sand, where now and then tan young people would come biking by, maybe roller blade past. Fremont ignored the guys and watched the young girls. Most were wearing short-shorts and halter-tops. A few, their young bodies toned, were wearing bikinis, even thongs. Shit. All were blonde—that's the way it seemed—all of them fast on wheels too, of some kind or another. It was something that he could get used to.

He was having trouble, however, shaking the feeling of being out of place. A part of him saying hallelujah, while another part kept expecting someone, maybe in uniform, to come by, ask him what the hell he was doing.

"Well, I'm just sittin' here thinkin' to jump the little white girls, they come gliding by. Is there a problem, Officer?"

He'd only been in town a month. Taking a job two days after arriving as a carpet cleaner in the San Fernando Valley. Something to do till he could get situated. It was that same old grind, the work he fell back on when he didn't have a score of some kind going.

Getting to know the bartender, Alejandro, at the Marriott in Canoga Park, he mentioned that he'd done some time for breaking and entering. Six months one time on a conviction, sentence reduced. A second time, twenty-four hours while awaiting formal charges—the witness misidentifying him in a second photo line-up, resulting in the charges being dropped—both County, no hard time. He said nothing about the city councilman that he and his buddy Lougie had dumped in the city landfill. That was then.

"Yeah?" Alejandro had said, responding to the idea and suddenly getting interested. He motioned him with a conspiratorial nod toward the end of the bar where it was private. "You looking for work?"

"Depends what kind of work," Fremont told him.

"There's this guy I know looking for someone don't mind getting his hands dirty, you know what I mean?"

"What I gotta do?" Fremont asked.

Alejandro had shrugged the question, saying, "Whatever he tells you. You interested?"

He hadn't given Fremont much more than that to go on. Like who the guy was, for starters, what he looked like. Hang out, Alejandro had told him, wait for a guy named

Winston to show up. Maybe he was supposed to walk up and down the beach askin' had anyone seen Winston lately.

Something else to make Fremont uneasy: the matter of what the job was the guy was supposed to be offering. A score of some sort, Fremont figured. Believing the guy maybe wanted him, in his capacity as carpet cleaner, to case the houses he was cleaning, or maybe wanted him to leave a patio door accidentally unlocked for a late night slip in—the guy maybe into home invasion. Okay, then imagining, in this unfamiliar setting, all sorts of sting operations in effect and seeing handcuffs being snapped around his wrists...

Shit! Sitting here, the beach, his mind working on him.

What he would have to do, he decided, was get rid of the heavy work shoes, the brown zip-up coveralls with his name stitched above the pocket. Do it soon. Make a run to Ron-Jon's, that surf shop advertised on, Christ, every goddamn billboard in town. Pick himself up some surf jams with the wild flowers and shit on them, go Californian. Maybe slip on a pair of Birkenstocks. Yeah, get used to sand between his toes.

It was a good image to hold onto, Fremont decided, waiting and wondering about the guy named Winston, and feeling, just now, here on the beach, he'd arrived in the real L.A. for the first time.

It was another ten minutes before a silver BMW sedan, looking sneaky the way it suddenly appeared, slipped into the lot and pulled in some eight or nine slots down from Fremont in the half-empty front row of spaces. A Wednesday. Not the kind of car Fremont would have expected for a home invasion specialist. But then maybe the stealing-shit business was better here on the west coast. Fremont could see, through tinted glass, the silhouette of one person in the car, a man behind the wheel, but couldn't make out any features.

Fremont watched the car, its engine still idling, trying to decide should he sit still and wait, or walk up, like in the movies, and ask the guy did he have a light. Finally the BMW's driver-side window came down under power, and an arm extended out the window to wave him over.

Fremont took a quick glance down toward the beach, seeing people self-involved—walking in the sand, inspecting shells, playing volleyball—then got up, dusting sand off his pants, and approached the car.

"You Winston?" Fremont asked.

The man observed him—a cautious look—before saying, "I don't know. Are you the guy?"

"Yeah, shit, whatever, man," Fremont said. "I'm the guy. I'm *your* guy. What are we talking about?"

"Maybe it would be best if you got in," the man said.

Fremont did his best shuffle-stride around the front of the car, letting his hand trail across the BMW's hood emblem, getting a frown from the guy as he came around to open the door and slide into the seat.

The guy, early forties, wasn't at all what Fremont had imagined, expecting some heavy-muscled Italian with a Jersey accent to show up. Instead, this guy was slim and angular, with Buddy Holly glasses sitting on a pointy nose. Studious, he was. He was wearing a golf cap and golf shirt with matching country club logos, though Fremont had to wonder could he swing a club with those skinny arms. He was one of those preppy types that were so tight-assed they made little whistling noises with their butt when they walked. The guy only glanced at him before turning his gaze off toward the beach, where the civilized world went about its business. After a moment, the guy said, "Alejandro tells me you are skilled at breaking into houses?"

"You asking do I know how to rob a place?" Fremont said.

The man turned to look at him for the first time and there was something strange about his eyes. What was it? He realized, then, the man had two different colored eyes—one was dark brown; the other was pale green, the color of margarita mix.

"Yes...!" the guy said, as though seeing the idea for the first time, "Yes, exactly, that's precisely what I want. A robbery. Can you do that?"

"Hey, shit, yeah, okay..." Fremont said with a shrug, not wanting to sound surprised or anxious.

"In fact," the man said, "I think I'd like the place thoroughly burglarized. Mattresses, cabinets, vanities, drawers. Take whatever you want...stereo, VCR, jewelry, whatever you usually take, I'm sure I don't have to tell you. But it should be convincing. A real burglary. But there's one thing, one thing in particular, I want you to be very careful with."

"What's that?" Fremont said.

"Gammy."

Fremont looked at the man. "Gammy?"

"Yes, my dear departed grandmother. Her ashes, you understand. I want you to get them and bring them to me."

"Get out," Fremont said. "She your grandma, how come you got to have someone steal her?"

The man dropped his head. "It's a long story. You see, my wife and I are going through a very difficult time in our marriage. She moved out unexpectedly a week ago and is causing me a great deal of trouble financially. But that's neither here nor there. My concern, just now, is my grandmother. In my wife's haste...or perhaps out of vindictiveness...she took Gammy's ashes with her. She doesn't answer her door and she doesn't return my calls. I'm afraid it may be over with the two of us, but I simply must get Gammy back."

Fremont looked the man over carefully. His palms were sweating, leaving moist imprints on the steering wheel. But his jaw was set, determined, his eyes level. Still, a grown man calling his dead grandmother's ashes "Gammy." Jesus. He said, "Let me get this straight. You want me to rob your wife's house..."

"Apartment," the man corrected.

"Uh-huh...okay, you asking me to rob your wife's *apartment*, take whatever I want and bring your grandmama's ashes to you? That's it? What do you want me to do with the rest of the stuff I take?"

"Do whatever you usually do. Use it, sell it, whatever. That can be part of your reward, plus I'll give you one thousand dollars when I have Gammy back safe in my hands."

Fremont took some time with it, letting it sink in. "A thousand dollars?"

"I guess if you're not interested..."

"Hold on," Fremont said. "I'm interested. Did I say I'm not interested?"

"Do we have a deal then?"

Fremont gave it another moment of thought, then said, "Hey, shit, let's get Gammy reunited with her loved ones."

"Good." He reached above the visor and took down a folded piece of paper, handed it to Fremont. "The address of the apartment is on there, as well as the address to my office. Bring the urn there, shall we say, Friday night, around eight p.m. I'll have your payment waiting, in cash."

Fremont stuffed the folded paper into his coveralls and reached for the door handle. He paused, halfway out. "What about the missus live there?" he said.

When the man didn't respond immediately, Fremont turned in his seat to look at him.

"I don't know. You're the thief, do what thieves do. But if it should happen she gets in the way, something dreadful happens..." The man shrugged.

Fremont considered, then stepped out, closing the door behind him. Man, crazy in love with his grandma, don't care shit about his wife.

The silver BMW backed from the space and crossed the lot to the exit on Pacific Coast Highway. It turned, heading south, and disappeared into traffic.

Fremont turned his gaze back toward the beach, where a girl's volleyball game had just started up—four of them jumping and jiggling and hammering the ball back and forth across the net, serious about it. One of them spiked the ball for a score. There was high-fiving and a lot of re-adjusting of sports bras before the pairs got set for the next serve. It was all too grand, Fremont thought. And, shit, a thousand dollars and all the goods he could steal. He said to himself, "Rescue Gammy, shit." Wacky-ass Californians. Yeah, he could get used to this.

That night Fremont called his pal Lougie in Tucson. "Man, you gotta get out here. People in L.A., they throw their money at you, then beg you to pick it up and take it, no shit."

Lougie told him he was happy. He'd taken a job as a repo man. Get to drive around all night waiting for a guy to get out of his car, then drive up and steal it out from under him. Legal. Told him he had something called a "back-and-grab," let him snatch the car without having to get out of the truck. "Sees his car disappearing out of the lot at the Seven-Eleven, you should see the guy's face, man."

"Yeah, but I'm talking money for nothing," Fremont said.

Fremont had left Lougie behind a month ago, sick of the desert and finally free. Jimmy Nuccio, the developer who had been holding an incriminating videotape over his and Lougie's head, had suffered a stroke. Guardian angel at work, and he knew he and Lougie both had seen enough shit in life to deserve one.

That surveillance tape, that documented the abduction and, okay, subsequent murder of one of Tucson's finest public servants, could have gotten them the death penalty. As it was, they'd gotten life with Nuccio, the man dangling the tape over them, as evidence of the crime, leveraging them and using them like his own personal slaves. "Get me some coffee, clean up that mess, pick up Mister Rich Fucking Asshole at the airport and drive him to the Sheraton." Shit, Fremont and his pal were looking at forever that way. But now—blessed fate—Nuccio's stroke had left him paralyzed and foaming at the mouth. Not much of a witness.

Fremont, doing a jimmy-juke on the man's office, recovered the tape. And, after stopping by Circle K for a quart of malt liquor, built a fire in the dry wash of the Santa Cruz River and invited Lougie for an Independence Day party.

Watching the video evidence disintegrate, Fremont had told Lougie he was thinking about getting a fresh start. "How about California, man, the Land of Opportunity?"

He was surprised when Lougie didn't jump all over the idea.

"What's the matter, little buddy? Can't be you're in love with this heat, shit."

As it turned out Lougie missed the work, claiming it was the best job he'd ever had. How hard was it to drive somebody around or run errands for Mister Jimmy? He hoped to find another like it.

Fremont guessed he had a point about the Nuccio job, but asked him, said, "Man, don't you ever want something more than just some shit-easy paycheck?"

When it was obvious Lougie didn't, Fremont said, "Well, I'll see you later, my man," and pointed his Chevy Impala west on I-10. That was a month ago. Now, here on the phone, he was telling Lougie about his easy new gig. "This place I'm tossing is in Venice Beach, my man. Rich folks live on the beach, understand what I'm saying? They don't just have TV sets. They have Home Entertainment Systems. And jewels, man, size of ostrich eggs. Understand what I'm saying?"

Lougie said, "Uh-huh." But added, "When you coming home?"

Fremont's pal still didn't get it.

Thursday afternoon, Fremont found himself outside the apartment in Venice Beach. He had to double check the address. The place looked nothing like he had imagined. Instead of the sprawling, glass-realmed beach house with a view he'd pictured in his mind, this apartment was down an alley, boxed in, where houses and multi-units were crammed shoulder-to-shoulder. Eleven-seventeen, the one he was looking for, sat on stilts above a four-slot carport, looking like an afterthought that relied on airspace for its place in the world. Shit, the ocean nowhere in sight.

Fremont ducked through the carport. Hearing voices approaching from down the alley, he paused beneath the wooden stairs that led upward to the apartment. A pair of longhaired teens appeared, trucking fast. They were wearing jams and T-shirts and had surfboards tucked beneath their arms. They talked loud and in a language Fremont didn't understand, everything being "gnarly" or "bitchin'" and "like, totally awesome." They passed down the alley and were gone. Fremont gave it a beat, then mounted the stairs, two at a time until he reached the wooden landing. Taking a look around, seeing rooftops and cluttered back yards, he gave the door a rap with his knuckles. When nothing stirred and no one responded, Fremont clicked a switchblade into place, passed it between the latch and the strike-plate, and the door pushed open. Easy. And once again, Fremont was struck with disbelief.

The apartment was all but empty.

Fremont slipped inside, easing the door shut behind him. There were a few loosely filled boxes in the corner, a mattress on the floor. The bedclothes were rumpled. There was a pair of jeans and a red knit top in a pile. Fremont crossed quietly to the far wall, where an oven and a sink—

what served as the kitchen—sat littered with cereal boxes
and used plastic dinnerware. The sink had a skirt around it
to hide the drain, little flowers in the print to dress up the
skirt. A window looked out and beyond. A closed door to his
right would be the can. All there was to the glorious beach
house he'd imagined.

"Steal anything you want," the man had said. Shit.
There was nothing to steal.

Well, there was still the matter of Gammy's ashes
and the thousand dollars, if he could still believe in that.
Had the man known the wife was here with nothing?

Fremont scanned the barren room. No bookshelves or
tables, no mantelpiece to display the old lady on, but— hey,
shit—a ceramic jar cocked and peeking from one of the
boxes. Fremont crossed to the box and freed the heavy urn
from among shoes, scarves, books, and framed photos. It
was white with scenes of soaring songbirds painted in blue,
making him think of Chinese dynasties and ancient
porcelain worth millions. Or could be a cookie jar from
Pottery Barn. Fremont tried the lid. It was sealed. He lifted
the urn above his head, tilted it to the light. An inscription
in the unglazed base read: *Dorchester Funeral Home.*

Fremont returned to the sink. He sat the urn amidst
the clutter. Then leaned on his knuckles and gazed out the
window to where more alleys and rooftops and backyards
could be seen, and a hazy blue horizon, off a mile or so, that
would be the Pacific. He thought about what Lougie would
say. Wondered about the best way to finish the story, make
it sound good, of the guy willing to pay a thousand dollars
for his dead grandmama's ashes, and how easy it was to
walk in and pick them up. He was still that way, off

someplace but to himself, when the door to the bathroom opened and a woman came into the room.

She was wrapped in a towel, cleavage showing above, and lots of bare white legs—nice legs—showing below. Still coming, she was drying her hair with another towel. Her head was tilted and she was still not seeing him. When she finally looked up, she stopped cold.

"Who are you?" she said. "What do you want?"

She looked surprised, Fremont thought—a girl in her mid-to-late twenties—the towel poised mid-ruffle. A frightened look on her face. He said, "Now don't get excited. I'm not here to hurt you."

She watched him carefully. "Then what do you want? You going to rob me? Go on. Take what you want. Take it all, does it matter?"

Fremont said, "Come on, shit."

The girl studied him for a moment then went back to work on her hair. "You a rapist? You don't look like a rapist."

How were you supposed to answer that?

As Fremont tried to think of a way to respond, the girl crossed to the mattress, where her jeans and top lay tossed in a pile. She pitched her head-towel, then, without so much as a hesitation, she slipped from her wrap and bent to retrieve her jeans. Jesus!

Fremont watched in awe as she stepped into the jeans. Watched further, as she skinnied them over the curve of her hips, snapped them tight at the waist, and zipped them closed.

She turned to him with the same bold candor, two of the most beautiful white breasts he'd ever seen looking straight at him, and pulled the top over her head. When she'd run fingers through her hair and tossed it out with a shake of her head, she said, "So what now? Do I call the cops or you going to leave on your own?"

The girl looked pretty fine in the jeans and the red top, with her hands on her hips. He could see that her hair was mostly blonde, highlights starting to show. He said, "How come all your stuff's gone?"

"It's what you get when you're married to the biggest loser of all time...wait a minute..." Her eyes narrowed on the urn, out of the box and sitting amid dishware on the sink. "He sent you, didn't he? My husband. That's what this is about. He sent you to recover his grandmother's ashes. Fucking mama's boy, I might have expected."

Fremont held her gaze, having a hard time, wanting more to scan the length of her body, said nothing.

Finally she said, "What the hell, take her. What am I going to do with the old bat anyway? I only took her to piss him off. You want a drink? I'm having one."

She crossed toward him, pushing past him now, to get to the cabinet above the stove.

Fremont watched as the girl stood on tiptoe to fish down a bottle of Jim Beam.

"I hope you like bourbon, Slick, it's all I've got."

As she poured rounds into a couple of plastic cups, she said, "You don't say much, do you?"

Fremont had to think about that one. His pal, Lougie would say he talked too much, complained about it. He thought, there's got to be things you could say, this situation. And still nothing was coming to him.

She handed a cup to him. Then, holding her cup extended, she said, "Well, Slick...wait, what's your name?"

"Fremont."

"Here's to us, Fremont. We both picked one dumb horse's ass to hitch our cart to." She tapped her cup to his and threw her drink back with a toss of her head. Then, taking the bottle with her, she crossed to the mattress and sat down. Propping pillows against the wall, she leaned back and poured herself another drink.

Fremont stole a sip of bourbon, never taking his eyes off her.

"Did you know my husband has his Masters from Harvard Business School? Summa cum laude. You know what summa cum laude means?"

Fremont shook his head.

"It means you'd have to be armless, legless, and headless not to make two hundred thousand a year and live, at least, Beverly Hills-adjacent. My husband," she said, "Mister Winston Gayle Magnuson the Third, Mister Egghead, Mister whoop-ti-doo Harvard whiz kid, starts his own accounting practice, has one client! One! Something Brothers Movers...nets just over eighty thousand a year, still making that much after years in business. Doesn't have enough motivation to go out and find at least one other goddamn client."

"Married him for money, huh?" Fremont said, sipping.

"Well, I didn't sign on for this. How was I supposed to know he was the cheapest man in the universe? You want to know where we live?"

Fremont was sure she was going to tell him but said, "Where?"

"El Segundo!" She said it like it explained everything. "A little bungalow—so small!—I'm surprised they bother to give it a mailing address."

The girl was swirling her drink angrily, watching the liquid churn into eddies inside the glass. She stopped swirling, then knocked back the entire contents in a single gulp.

Fremont considered the girl's life: the bare walls, the cramped bathroom he could make out through the open doorway, the sorry collection of personal belongings gathered in just three boxes in the—sum total of her existence. He said, "There must have been something you could take with you."

"What, the furniture? Crap so outdated the man's grandma didn't want to sit on it when she was still alive."

Fremont sipped his drink, believing he should just tuck Gammy under his arm and go. He considered the idea of crawling up next to her on the mattress, too, and seeing where it led—this good looking blonde girl with the slim legs that went all the way to the floor. But he was trying to stay focused. The girl seemed open-minded, yeah, maybe a bit loose. And man, having her sweet self beneath him would be fine. On the other hand, if he slid his hand beneath her little red top and the girl started screamin'... shit...he'd be putting a thousand dollars at risk and maybe be looking at trumped up rape charges. He was about to make his excuses, when the girl said, "You know, there is one thing my husband has of value."

Fremont looked at her. She had her drink poised at her lips, where a mischievous grin had formed.

"Yeah...? What's that?" Fremont asked.

"He has this two-hundred-fifty-thousand dollar life insurance policy."

She continued grinning, letting the idea hang there for a long, weighty moment, then took a sip from her cup.

"Uh-huh..." Fremont said. He could already see where this was headed.

"Well, I was just thinking . . . if someone . . . let's say someone with nerve enough to walk into someone else's apartment unannounced, took it upon himself to have something terrible happen to poor Winston . . . then that other someone might just be grateful enough to share some of that new found wealth. Let's say . . . ten thousand dollars grateful."

"You paying me to kill your husband?"

"I suppose it would take a greater level of nerve than just breaking and entering. Maybe you're not interested."

"I could be interested. Did I say I wasn't interested?"

"Ever kill anyone before?"

"It's not something you go spreading around," Fremont said. He was picturing the city councilman he and Lougie tossed in the dump, with grubs and the like dining on what was left of his carcass.

"Then you have."

Fremont gave the idea some thought. Deliver Gammy's ashes, collect the grand. Then pop the man on the way out, come back, collect ten more. He shrugged, said, "How I know you'll give me the money you get it? I mean, how am I supposed to know I can trust you?"

There was that mischievous grin again, spreading across the girl's face. Her eyes had a dark twinkle in them. She set her drink aside, then lifted her gaze to look directly at him. Patting the mattress next to her, she said, "I guess we'll just have to work on our credibility."

That evening, Fremont had a new story to tell Lougie. "Man, we went all day long. She a blonde...did I mention she a blonde?"

Lougie told him they had blondes in Tucson, though he'd never personally had one.

Fremont asked him, said, "If you had ten...no, make that eleven thousand dollars...how many could you have then?"

Lougie said he didn't know what blondes went for these days. But asked in a reverent tone, "You've got eleven thousand dollars?"

"Well, no, not actually, yet..." Fremont admitted, but reminded Lougie California was, as he'd previously stated, the land of opportunity. "It's like heaven, man, 'cept they got air you can't see through and something they call Sig Alerts."

It was Friday, dark setting in, Fremont drove to Culver City and began looking for the address of Winston's office. Strapped in on the passenger seat next to him was the man's grandma.

"...thirty-eight, forty-three..." Reading the numbers above the storefronts. "What do you think, Gammy, you gonna be upset with me I pop your boy Winston? Yeah, shit, what do you care, huh?"

It was fully dark by the time Fremont found the address on Overland. His momentum carried him past the empty space at the curb and he had to drive another six blocks or so up the divided boulevard before getting the chance to turn around. Man! Land of opportunity making you work.

He parked where gold lettering on the window identified the office as Magnuson Accounting. The lights were out inside, the place looking closed or abandoned. Maybe Winston was playing it cool, not wanting anyone to see him with the man who'd just committed a break-in on the wife's apartment. No mention of breaking-in the wife herself while he was there. He decided to leave Gammy strapped in, safe on the street, until he could determine if Winston was in.

At the front door, blinds and deep darkness made it impossible for Fremont to tell if anyone was inside. He knocked—one light rap. The door gave way beneath his knuckles. Cautiously, he eased the door open.

All was quiet in the small foyer that Fremont found himself in. In the dim light that filtered through the door from the street, he saw straight-back chairs and the outlines of framed pictures on the wall—a cramped waiting room. Nothing fancy.

Easing the door shut, he made his way down a short hallway that led to an office at the back. There in the muted glow of a toppled desk lamp, Fremont found Winston sprawled in his chair...

Hey, shit!

There were two holes in the man's chest, blood spreading across his tweed vest. More blood ran from one empty socket where the brown eye used to be. The other eye, the green one, still there, stared back at him.

Fremont righted the lamp, carefully using his cuff to grip the stem. In the broader circle of light, now, he could tell the room had been tossed. Papers were strewn about the floor, desk drawers were scattered, file cabinets had been rifled and overturned. The computer's monitor had been dashed to the floor, smashed to a thousand bits in, what looked to Fremont, an act of frustration. Someone looking for something they hadn't found.

He examined the papers on the floor. Some were letters with the Magnuson letterhead. But many looked like computer generated ledger pages, ripped and torn and pitched to the wind. The headings read: "Salvatore Brothers Rigging and Moving."

No, shit! Fremont thought. He remembered the girl saying her husband had had only one customer. Now the man was dead. All shot up and nowhere to go. And whoever had killed him had done so execution style.

In the blink of an eye, Fremont realized, he had gone from collecting one thousand dollars and counting on ten more, to being out gas money from all the running around he was doing, and wondering if the girl would technically have to pay him. The husband, Winston, was dead, after all, Fremont reasoned. Did the girl have to know it wasn't Fremont who killed him?

Fremont tipped the lamp back on its side and turned quickly toward the exit. Outside, he slid behind the wheel of his Impala. "I don't know how to break it to you, Gammy," he told the urn, as he fired the engine, "but little Winston's dead."

Fremont punched the Impala and held the accelerator to the floor. It was twenty minutes to Venice Beach.

Fremont rehearsed his way back to the girl's apartment, running lines with Gammy on the seat beside him. "It was like this," Fremont told the ashes, "I broke in and shot the man, execution style, two in the chest, one in the... no, that makes the death sound like a contract killing, she may get nervous and not pay up." Gammy didn't say anything, so Fremont said. "Okay, I broke in, shot the man, then tossed the place good, make it look like a burglary gone bad. Much better."

He could have saved his breath.

Gammy wasn't listening, and when Fremont arrived at the apartment, he found the place empty. Not just sparse, like before, but empty. The young wife, and all signs of her had vanished in the night. If she'd ever planned to pay him, Fremont wasn't sure. His guess was, no. She'd sent him on a mission with a promise, and then cleared out, making sure she was as far away from whatever transpired as possible. To her thinking, Fremont reasoned, the man would either be dead, or he wouldn't. Simple. Now she had her wish, two-hundred-fifty-thousand-dollars richer, and Fremont was going home with a dead woman's ashes on the front seat.

That night, Fremont avoided calling Lougie. Instead he bought a bottle of Chivas Regal and got drunk with Gammy, telling her all about Arizona and what a great place it was to live. "You should try it, you'll see. Maybe I'll take you there sometime," he said, slurring his words and squinting at the little bluebirds that seemed to be in motion about the urn. "Like the song says, 'If you want to be happy for the rest of your life, always make an older woman your wife . . . ' no wait . . . I think it said 'ugly . . . make an ugly woman . . .' hey, shit, what's the difference. Me and you, Gammy, what do you say, girl?"

When morning came Fremont made his mind up to return to Arizona, a place where work and life just weren't this hard. He had, however, given up on taking Gammy back with him. She really wasn't much of a conversationalist and couldn't be much for sex, her condition. So he drove out to Palos Verdes where he'd seen cliffs overlooking the ocean.

It was a fitting farewell, dust the old lady off the side of the cliff, then use what cash he had left to return to the desert.

On the cliffs—million dollar estates at his back—Fremont could look down on the surf, breaking white against the rocks. He could see the island of Catalina in a far-off haze out on the horizon. His dream of the good life had become as wispy as the marine layer that clouded his view. "Well, hey, shit, Gammy, it's been fun," he told the urn, gripping it beneath one arm to twist the top free of its seal.

His story for Lougie, he decided, would be to tell him that, man, he just had to get away, this place, before the young California ladies wore him out. "I had to come back just to get some rest, shit," he'd say.

It was lame, but it would have to do.

Fremont tipped the urn and let Gammy's ashes scatter on the updraft. He watched them drift to the surf below. By way of eulogy, he said, "There you go, old Gammy-girl. Knock one off in the afterlife for me."

Fremont might have tossed the urn over, as well, if not for an instinct to check it and make sure all of Gammy had departed. As it was, the ashes were all gone, but what remained was a folded piece of paper, caught on the rim of the jar. Fremont tweezed it free with his fingers, dusted it off, and examined its content. There on the page was a long list of banks—names like *Freeport Swiss National Bank, Zurich-Grand Bahamas Mercantile*. Next to them were lengthy account numbers...offshore accounts, Fremont realized...and a column with dollar amounts. Jesus, Mary and Joseph! More than twenty million dollars.

Yeah, now it figured. The Salvatore Brothers, maybe mob connected, had whacked their lackey accountant and went bugshit in the office looking for these. Millions in funds siphoned, perhaps a bit at a time, from mob revenues and diverted into numbered accounts by the egghead, whoop-ti-doo, college whiz-kid, Winston Gayle Magnuson the Third. Fremont thought of the man's wife—young, attractive, Christ, a hellcat in bed, but impatient and hell-bent on prosperity—running out on the man for his doltishness, not knowing he'd been secretly building a fortune out of mob money.

"Get out, shit! Millions?" Fremont said aloud, reading and re-reading the seven-digit dollar signs. "You rich, motherfucker!" he told himself. Then thought, Shit!...the pass code. How was he going to get the dead fuck's pass code?

It took Fremont only a minute before he came to reason: a man like Winston, so wrapped up in his grandmother, could have only one possible code. Five little letters, beginning in G and ending in Y. Freemont smiled. It had to be. Either way, he decided, there were millions of dollars sitting unclaimed. He'd find a way.

Freemont looked out across the far horizon. He wanted to cry, but didn't know how. He turned to look inland at the million dollar homes, the manicured lawns, the extravagance, and realized how possible it had all suddenly become. He began to laugh...then the tears came. He would call Lougie, after all, he thought, snuffling. But not right away. Not for a few days. And not until he had actually gone to sleep and woken up to find out he wasn't just dreaming.

"Thank you, Lord," Fremont whispered, remembering the guardian angel. Then revised his prayer to include a thank you to Gammy—the old girl who had passed the numbers on to him.

He wouldn't be going back to Arizona, Fremont concluded. Not now. But he would have a story for Lougie. A good one. About making it with Gammy...and about the land of opportunity.

*In the heart of Los Angeles lies the historic **Biltmore Hotel**. Although the city skyline has evolved to include modern steel and glass towers, the grand dame of downtown continues to hold court on Pershing Square. Designed in a Beaux Arts style with Renaissance Revival touches, the Biltmore opened with great fanfare in 1923 and instantly became the 'toast of the coast.' Over the decades, this bastion of old-world charm and elegance has housed presidents, kings, and Hollywood elite. Most people would recognize the original lobby with its spectacular Moorish beamed ceiling and giant Spanish baroque staircase, a popular backdrop for numerous Hollywood movies and TV shows. People from all walks of life pass through this lobby—the raucous conventioneer, the weary business traveler, and sometimes the master criminal. As you sip your martini at the lobby bar, keep an eye out. You might catch a glimpse of someone slipping behind a potted palm and through an exit that leads to murder...*

MARATHON MADNESS
by Dee Ann Palmer

I drummed my fingers on the counter at the concierge's desk in the historic Biltmore Hotel in downtown Los Angeles, waiting for the DASH schedule. For a small fee, the little bus shuttles people around the downtown area. For the running of the City of Los Angeles Marathon, the first weekend in March, it carries visitors to and from their hotels to the Expo at the Convention Center for free. That's where runners pick up their race number bibs and goodie bags.

While I waited, I studied the American Beauty roses on the counter. Their scent under the arch of the carved, wooden ceiling was sweet and inviting. Turning, I saw how their color picked up flecks of red in the area rug's blend of green, gold, aqua, and blue in the center of the lobby. Noticing the rug I'd just walked across made me conscious that my ragged running shoes weren't up to such elegance, and I felt embarrassed that I hadn't worn something different.

While I contemplated my shoes, someone bumped me. Glancing up, I saw that Janet Widlow, one of my least favorite persons, had backed into me. If I turned away, I wouldn't have to speak to her, but she turned instead and spoke first.

"Oh, it's you. You're in my running club, right?"

Great. Now I'd have to talk to her or be rude. I watched her look at me, squinting her dark eyes, which I'd like to call beady because it perfectly describes what I think of her, but they aren't beady, so I won't. I could see her thoughts churning as surely as if she had a glass head.

Finally, she said, "You're..."

"Suevee Taylor." I decided not to extend my hand.

"Oh, yes, the one with the strange name. You staying here?"

I nodded. "And you?"

"Eighth floor."

"We're in 423." Immediately, I regretted giving out our number. The less contact I had with this unpleasant woman, the better.

"You with Anna?"

Just like that, I was dismissed. A little tinge of irritation pulled at me. My dear friend Anna Hillman, tall and lean and, like Janet, built to run, had developed a stress fracture in her right foot two weeks ago. Seven months of training for a marathon, and suddenly the orthopedic surgeon, who usually advises taking ibuprofen and going ahead, says, "No running for six weeks."

I told Janet as much.

"Good thing she's not here. I'd beat her."

Humility. That's what I've always admired about this woman. She's the only one in our age group in the club who's ever beaten Anna, and then only once. The next time they raced, and Janet came in second, she'd had nothing but excuses for why she hadn't won.

"Where you headed?" she asked.

"The Convention Center."

"Ride with me. I'm driving a Maserati Spyder."

Oh, sure. Wheel up in an expensive sports car, top down, so Janet could show off the car and a "friend." Not on your life.

"Thanks, but Hal's with me. I assume the Spyder only seats two? We'll take the DASH."

"You still with that NFL has-been?"

She wasn't joshing me, and I recognize envy when I hear it. Me she didn't remember; Hal she did. An image of the powerful build and rugged face of the man who was my seriously significant other, sprang to mind. *Has-been*, indeed. Something naughty jingled inside me. "I doubt you know any man who's on the gridiron winning Super Bowl rings at our age, Janet, but yeah, I'm still with a man who won two of them in his day."

As I expected, she was impervious to the sarcasm.

She shrugged, her face expressionless. "So you prefer DASH to a Maserati. Suit yourself."

The concierge handed me the schedule. Janet was still by my side as we left the lobby and stepped into the corridor that led to the gift shop, bar, health center, and various ballrooms. She started up the steps to the elevator landing while I looked around for the door to the stairs.

"You aren't coming?"

"Elevators aren't my thing."

Framed by perfectly coiffed blonde hair, scorn was written all over her carefully made up face. I felt no urgency to explain I'd been trapped in an elevator down in Florida during a hurricane. It had been a long four hours before we were freed. Just the sight of an elevator these days makes me anxious.

"Later then." As she moved past me she said, with a dismissive wave of her hand, "I'm going to beat you."

"Yeah, well, good luck to you too," I called cheerily. "Maybe I'll see you at the Convention Center." *Not. I hope.*

I wondered how people like Janet, who scored zilch when it came to social skills, got along in life. Regarding her remark about Hal being a has-been, Anna would have said, "Oh, that's just her idea of humor among friends."

I didn't think so.

* * *

I'm Susan Valencia Taylor—Suevee to my friends—and I'm a marathoner. Female, age 50-54 division, average height for a woman and not as slender as Anna and Janet. I've run Walt Disney World, St. George, Las Vegas, Boston, and Portland, but there's nothing like doing L. A.

Born and bred in a neighborhood on the north side of the Hollywood Park Racetrack, I love Los Angeles. Hal and I live inland now, deep in Orange County, but when I return to run this marathon I feel like I'm coming home. The skyline has changed since I left. They've built Staples Center and the multi-towered Bonaventure Hotel, but my heart, my childhood joys belong to these streets.

The Biltmore, the most famous hotel ever built in Los Angeles, offers special rates to marathoners. I adore it. I'm a walking tour guide. I can tell you that construction on the 170 foot high-rise was completed in 1923, and there are 683 guest rooms, fifty-six suites, and thirteen floors above ground.

Breathe in the air, touch the walls, walk the parquet floors, cross the carpets, and you feel the whisper of old wealth and history. It's marvelous.

One thing I did not know was where to find the entrance to the stairs. As I hunted for it, I saw a waiter coming out of one of the ballrooms. Through the open doorway I could see them flinging pink linens over tables and setting them with gleaming crystal and china. Lush centerpieces were added last. Busboys and waiters in black trousers, maroon cummerbunds, starched white shirts, and short black jackets were coming and going from somewhere nearby.

The waiter walked over to a middle-aged busboy who was dark and swarthy, and seemed to berate him for some transgression. The swarthy man scowled and turned away. The waiter moved in my direction.

"What are they setting up for?" I asked.

"Wedding reception." He smiled. English was obviously not his first language. He looked Mexican.

"It's beautiful," I said.

"Persian," he answered.

"Ah, Persian." I smiled knowingly. When I asked about the stairs, he asked for my room number and I told him.

"Then you will wish to take this staircase," he said as he pointed to a nearby door over which the words "Stairs" appeared in small letters.

"*Gracias.*"

His face widened in a smile. "*De nada,*" he replied.

Today Persia is Iran. I know a runner married to an Iranian. She'd told me of the wealth among the Persians and the fabulous weddings she'd attended. I hoped I'd get a glimpse of this reception at some point.

But now my thoughts returned to the race. This year some anonymous Mr. or Ms. Rich Pockets gave our running club the money to refund the entry fee of anyone who comes in first in their age division. At sixty bucks a hit, most of us considered that a goal worth aiming for.

Anna is Janet's toughest competitor. I usually come in third, but with Anna out of the picture, I'm now Widlow's competition tomorrow for the club money.

I finally located the door and entered the poorly lit stairwell. The door closed behind me, shutting out the sounds of the reception preparations to leave a silence that was surreal.

The deserted staircase was wide and winding, with a graceful wrought iron railing. In the Biltmore's heyday, before its renovation in the 1980s, it must have been the grand staircase. I mounted it slowly at first, thinking the soft, mint colored carpet, a color I loved, had to be new because yarn fuzz had collected on each edge of the steps. Then I noticed a fine layer of dust coating them. The only marks were a single set of ascending footprints, large enough for a man.

The silence, the dust, and how perplexed the concierge had been when I asked where the stairs were, as if no one ever asked, doubled my uneasiness. A female acquaintance of mine had been attacked recently in a place like this. Suddenly feeling very vulnerable, I practically ran up the final steps to our landing. I was glad Hal and I were staying only four flights up.

Despite my claustrophobia, the elevator was looking better and better to me.

"There's a thirty per cent chance of showers tomorrow," Hal said as he switched off the weather channel.

"No problem." I stood on tiptoe to kiss his cheek. "Hmm, you smell good. Let me waterproof my shoes before we go to the Expo."

His quarterback hands encircled my waist as securely as they had handled a football, and he hugged me to him as his lips touched mine. "Just don't spray them in here, okay?"

As tough as Hal is, he's sensitive to odors, and waterproofing is one of the smells that turns his stomach.

I took my New Balances to a short hall that led to an outdoor landing. These were new shoes, carefully broken in, soft enough not to cause blisters but new enough to have cushioning and stability. Mine were just right. I held my breath against the acrid smell as I sprayed my shoes and left them in the hall to dry until we returned from dinner.

Hal coaxed me into the elevator. "Just the two of us alone," he whispered in a voice that made my mouth tingle. He nipped my ear. "I think we could figure out how to pass the time if we were stranded, don't you?"

Despite the tight ball of anxiety in my throat, the elevator slipped smoothly to the ground floor and opened. I relaxed.

We headed for the corridor that went past the reception ballroom, but I grabbed Hal's arm and stopped him. I'd spotted Janet talking to the swarthy busboy I'd seen the waiter scold earlier. I only saw the back of her, but she seemed tense. He in turn was waving his arms at her and glowering as he talked.

I chuckled. No doubt she'd upset the man with her imperious manner. Of course, he didn't seem so pleasant either. I grabbed Hal's arm. "There's Janet. Let's not go this way."

"Where?" Hal had never met her.

"Arguing with that busboy, I think. I don't want to have to introduce you. Frankly, I don't think even you could charm that woman."

Hal laughed, and we exited through the front entrance and caught DASH.

* * *

Hundreds of people came and went at the Expo. It was huge, vendors hawking their wares of brightly colored runner's clothing, energy bars and drinks, little blue and white packages of Biofreeze gel samples to apply to injuries during the race. There must have been a hundred people ahead of me in the line to pick up bib numbers, tee shirts, and goodie bags.

"Got your timing chip?" Hal asked when I finally turned away with my bag.

I reached inside and pulled it out along with a narrow red strip of cloth to Velcro it to my shoe. The chip's timer wouldn't activate until I crossed the electronic mat at the start line. It would shut down when I hit the finish line mat. Even if it took ten minutes to get to the starting line, the chip would know my actual race time from start to finish. Chips were turned in at the close of the race, but the Velcro strip was yours. Marathoners keep them on their shoes as a statement of pride: *I* run marathons.

* * *

When we returned to the Biltmore, the bride and groom were arriving for their reception. Her dress of white satin was covered with pearl and crystal beadwork, and her ladies in waiting were removing a frothy train that must have trailed ten feet behind her during the ceremony. She wore a heavy parure of what might be rubies and diamonds set in platinum and gold. They gleamed richly under the bright lights and complemented her dark coloring with perfection. I fantasized that the parure was an antique, a gift from the groom – passed down through generations in his family. His black tuxedo mirrored his dark hair and eyes, and his snowy shirt cuff slipped up to reveal a Rolex watch I suspected had not been bought from a street vendor.

"Wow," Hal whispered.

"Uh huh," I said. "Everyone in that room is dressed to the nines."

It was as my friend had said. The women wore long gowns of satin, crepe, or layered chiffon decorated with sequins and beads. Their ears, fingers, and necks dripped with what I imagined to be emeralds, diamonds, sapphires, and pearls.

I drank in the splendor of it all. It was so *Biltmore,* so nostalgically *L. A.* Such a treasure to see.

The doors closed behind the bride and groom, and we moved to the elevator, shutting that different, glittering world out of our minds.

Back in our room I pinned my race number on my running shirt. There's nothing worse than arriving at the start line only to discover you've left your race number in the hotel.

Like many distance runners, I'm plagued by an irritable gut that requires I eat with care before long runs. My breakfast, taken two hours before a race, is a high protein, high carbohydrate drink. It's safe to have a hamburger the night before a long race, and Hal was good enough to agree to a high fat meal at a Jack in the Box two blocks away.

I'm not good company the night before a marathon. My mind is preoccupied with race strategy and the course. I was reviewing every hill, every landmark, and calculating when to go and when to slow. Already I was trying to psyche myself into not starting too fast. That never works. Knowing I was bad company, I reached for Hal's hand as soon as we were on the street just to let him know I was still connected to him. You don't find drive-thrus in downtown L. A., and we sat down to a leisurely meal of cheeseburgers, shakes, and french fries.

Afterwards, we decided to walk uphill on Olive a block, past the hotel to the restaurants and offices on California Plaza. Small geysers spring out of the ground in the Watercourt, where children play in the summer. All of this is new since my childhood. The upper station to Angel's Flight is there, and I wanted to ride it. This small funicular with two counterbalanced passenger cars ascending and descending the hill, was originally built at the turn of the century. Billed as the shortest railway in the world, it connected the steep drop from the posh Victorian mansions on Bunker Hill with the Broadway retail district below. After World War II, Bunker Hill became a slum. The lovely Victorian homes were razed or converted to boarding houses. In the 1960s, the area became an urban renewal project, and Angel's Flight was dismantled with the expectation it would be rebuilt in a "couple" of years. It reopened in 1996.

Then one of the cars slipped. Seven people were injured. One person died.

I had forgotten. We stood at the archway and looked down to the one below. Once again, the cars had been removed. The deserted tracks created a melancholy that ruined my reverie.

"Let's go back to the hotel," I told Hal, as a shudder swept through me.

* * *

When we arrived at the entrance to the Biltmore, three black and whites were parked there.

"What have we here?" Hal said.

In the lobby, a uniformed officer told us the corridor leading to the bridal reception ballroom was off limits.

We turned away, but I was curious about what had happened. "Let's ask the concierge," I said.

She was young, and her badge read "Concierge in Training." I was relieved because I thought the regular concierge might not have answered our questions.

She said, "A wedding reception guest forgot to put on a very expensive necklace and earrings she'd laid out. When she realized it, she immediately left to retrieve it, but the set was gone. The wall safe in the closet had been pried open and some money was missing. We're suggesting everyone check their rooms."

Hal slipped his arm around my shoulder as we went up the steps to the elevator landing. We stood there, our backs to the elevators, looking down on a second lobby and the large glass doors opening onto 5th Street.

"Anyone could walk in off the street from there or leave by that route quickly," Hal said.

A muted ding signaled the arrival of the elevator. When we reached our floor, we stepped out into an empty corridor.

Back in the room, I began to lay out my race gear. "Oh my gosh, my shoes. I need to fasten my chip onto my shoes."

I went out to retrieve them, walking down the corridor to the short hallway where I'd left them.

The hall was empty.

I went to the end and opened the door to the outside landing. Nothing.

"Did you bring in the shoes I sprayed?" I asked Hal when I'd returned to the room.

He shook his head.

"Then someone stole them." I sank onto the bed, shaking my head in disbelief, stomach roiling. You'd have to be an athlete to understand the importance of shoes to a runner. Your feet are everything. The first year Mark Platjes was expected to win he had to drop out at mile ten because he'd forgotten his orthotics. "I can't believe someone stole my shoes."

Hal stood up. "Let's check again."

We cruised the entire corridor to the elevator and back. Nothing.

"Maybe," I said, "That theft wasn't just for jewelry. Maybe there's someone who stalks the corridors looking for things like this." The hotel had other guests staying here, but so far we hadn't seen anyone on this floor.

Now I had something else to think about—running in old shoes. Thankfully, I'd brought them, but they had broken down. Without their usual cushioning, I'd finish the race with the bottoms of my feet burning. I might get blisters that would make it impossible for me to finish. At worst, I could end up with stress fractures.

I was a very unhappy camper.

In bed, in the darkness, I felt Hal reach for me.

I grew rigid. "I thought they didn't allow that sort of thing before your NFL games."

He stroked my arm, his fingers strong yet gentle. "Come on, baby, you're tied up in knots. Roll over so I can get to your back."

Reluctantly, I let him knead the knots out of my shoulders and long muscles.

And when it went to other things, well, I had a little hint that the pre-game rules hadn't always been followed in the NFL. I drifted to sleep feeling loose and satisfied.

* * *

He was asleep the next morning when I leaned to kiss him goodbye.

"Break a leg," he mumbled.

I swatted him across his still-tight butt. "Thanks a lot."

Out front, I caught a crowded shuttle to the starting line on Figueroa, not far from the Coliseum. Excitement drifted through the little bus like ozone after a lightning strike.

"At least it isn't raining," a young woman behind me said.

"Maybe it will before everyone finishes, but right now it's perfect. Cool and moist." This from a man whose thin jersey tank top and skimpy shorts promised to leave him chilled once he began to sweat.

Dressed in the pink T-shirt of my running club and black running skins, I thought I'd be more comfortable. The marathon begins at 8:45 a.m., and that can be too late if it's hot. I was glad it wasn't warm today, but I was still steamed about my theft.

"Someone stole my shoes," I said. "If it rains before I finish, these old ones will give me blisters for sure."

Sympathetic nods and exclamations boosted my morale.

Once off the shuttle, I forced my way through a frightening crush of bodies into the four-hour finishing time block, greeting several members of my running club. I could already smell body odor created by nervous tension, and the feel of so many people crowded around me began to make me nervous too.

There was no sign of Janet. There were probably 25,000 runners in this competition. She could be ahead of or behind me and still win. I shook out my arms and legs to loosen up.

Don't worry about her. Concentrate on running your own race.

The gun went off.

Every chip that crossed the mat at the start line caused it to sing. I felt my blood singing in answer.

Due to the mass of runners, only the elite runners, cordoned off ahead of the rest of us so they had plenty of room, were able to actually run at this point. We peons were well past the second block before we could do more than walk.

A marathon is 26 miles, 385 yards long. Anything can happen in the race. I never knew if or when my body might betray me with cramps, knee injuries, dehydration, or friction that rubbed my inner thighs raw or blistered my feet. The first man who ran this distance, from Marathon to Athens to report that the Greeks had conquered the Persians, collapsed and died. Of course, no one knows why the man died, but the joke among marathoners was that he obviously hadn't trained for seven months as we did to run that far.

Adrenalin hyped me up. I started too fast. When I saw the blue and gray Mile Five banner that hung above and across the street, I checked my watch and knew I had to slow down. I didn't want to repeat the experience of the first marathoner.

The lines for the portable potties were long, and I turned one corner to see eight men standing in a row, eight golden streams wetting the side of an office wall. I shook my head and ran on. It was unfair that women didn't have that option.

At mile thirteen, I walked through a water stop, carefully avoiding a banana peel, greedily drinking from cups volunteers handed us. Next to me, a red-haired young man, face flushed and sweat dripping off his chunky body, looked at his watch. "I guess we didn't win the Hondas."

"No laurel wreaths for our heads either," I said.

By mile fifteen, we had also missed the wedding of three runners who'd passed us earlier. Bride and groom wore hip length wedding gear, running shorts, and Nikes. Even the officiating judge was in a short robe and running gear.

The bottoms of my feet felt like two hot coals.

It was at the mile sixteen water stop, when fatigue was signaling I might "hit the wall," that I felt someone shove something into my left hand. It was soft and heavy, and when I glanced down I saw a black velvet bag, its silk drawstrings pulled tight. Looking around to see who might have passed the thing to me, I saw Widlow weaving through runners a quarter of a block ahead. Where on earth had she come from? And...I gasped...she was wearing my shoes!

Anger surged through me. I always mark the backs of my shoes heavily with permanent marking pen so I can tell mates and when I'd bought them. She'd stolen my shoes!

I took another gulp of water, ready to increase my speed and catch up to her, but a runner bumped into me and almost knocked me down. Water hit my windpipe. Choking and coughing, I stopped. I couldn't run if I couldn't breathe. I fought mentally to stop coughing and relax the spasms in my voice box so air could get through.

People slapped me on the back, which was no help, and I raised a hand signaling them to stop.

Finally, I could breathe and run again. By now Janet was out of sight. I took the last bit of water just as a man slammed into me hard and fast. I choked and the coughing and gasping for air began all over again.

"You okay?" a man asked as he ran in place beside me. "That guy isn't even entered in the race. No bib, and none of the rest of us are running that fast."

I nodded and waved him on.

My hand closed tight around the velvet bag. Had Janet shoved it into my hand? If she had I didn't know why, but it's a jungle out there, and I am not stupid. You don't keep anything someone shoves into your hand, pocket or suitcase. I veered off to a side street, hunting for and finally finding a thick bush. I jammed the bag in to hide it, noting the street name. If she'd passed the bag to me and didn't have a good explanation after the race, I'd notify the police.

My foray onto the side street had added to her edge on me. If I hadn't been so tired, I'd have sprinted to catch up and find out now if she'd handed me that bag and why in hell she had on my shoes.

A few miles later, when we were on Hollywood Boulevard, I heard screams from Grauman's Chinese Theatre, and saw runners dashing over to it. As fatigued as I was, as much as my feet hurt, I couldn't resist investigating. I knew celebrities had signed and pressed their hand prints in cement squares in the Forecourt of the Stars, but why were people screaming? I'd lost precious seconds anyway, so I entered the court and slowed to running in place.

Maybe I expected to see a celebrity, maybe a Chinese dragon twisting and turning its huge head as it danced through the court. What I did not expect to see was a female runner lying crumpled on her back in one corner. A woman who'd just felt her pulse shook her head and stepped away. In an instant I took in the pale face against the red pool on the gray cement and wondered irrationally on which star's hand prints she'd fallen. Her eyes stared upward as if admiring the coral columns that held up the bronze pagoda roof, but they were glazed over. I didn't think they'd ever see anything again. Someone had grabbed her from behind, slit her throat, and left her to die on the streets of L. A.

It was Janet Widlow.

Bile rose in my throat. "Who has a cell phone? Call 911!"

They say that women do what needs to be done and later fall apart. Men supposedly fall apart and then pull themselves together. They also say hearing's the last sense to go. Instinctively, I crouched and touched her shoulder. "It's Suevee, Janet. Paramedics are on their way. Hang in there."

"We should move back," the pulse-taking runner said. "We're in a crime scene."

The paramedics arrived in four minutes. I waited for them, sensing it was too late for CPR.

It was.

I turned to the medic taking notes. "I know her, but I didn't see what happened. In case the police want to talk to me, I'd like to leave you my name and where I'm staying."

They rerouted us away from the theatre. I broke into a run, but all the fun out of "doing L.A." had evaporated.

* * *

Hal was waiting for me just outside the crush of the finish line photography and food section. I hobbled toward him barefoot, a finisher's medal on a red, white, and blue ribbon hanging from my neck, my wasted shoes in one hand.
"How'd you do?"
"I won the club competition. Janet's dead."
Then I burst into tears.

* * *

For the third time, I told the two homicide detectives who were interviewing me in the Biltmore manager's office, "I don't know who handed me the bag. I just know I saw Janet for the first time in the race just after someone shoved it into my hand. As my left hand swung down, someone pushed it into my hand. I glanced down to see what it was, then I saw Janet weaving her way through runners about a block ahead of me.

"I didn't open the bag; I don't know what was inside. All I could think of was to get rid of it. What if it had drugs in it? Besides, someone stole my shoes last night, and Janet was wearing them. She knew our room number, and she'd stolen my running shoes. I wasn't going to let her win the club prize if she'd stolen my shoes."

I itched from dried sweat on my skin. My ponytail had come loose, and my hair hung in dark wet clumps about my head. The leather couch on which I was sitting was cold. I began to shiver.

The heavier of the two men, Detective McAnally, removed his jacket and put it around my shoulders. It smelled of cigarette smoke. The odor nauseated me.

"Thanks. Can someone get me something to eat? I need food." Fatigue was setting in, and my blood sugar needed a boost.

"She was driving a Maserati Spyder?"

"That's what she said. Offered me a ride, but I didn't like her and I was with Hal so I didn't accept. I didn't see her in a car. Any car. I saw her in the front lobby, then again in the corridor near the bridal reception, once running, once dead. That's all." My voice shook. The image of her body reeled through my mind again like a silent horror movie. Tears welled up in my eyes, threatening to roll down my cheeks. I managed to hold them back so they drained down my ducts into my nose and throat.

"You didn't report your missing shoes even though you knew a theft was being investigated. Even though you'd been advised to check your things."

I wiped my nose and shook my head. "They were just running shoes. If Janet forgot hers she may have come up to see if I had an extra pair, spotted those and taken them. They weren't in front of our room. No room doors opened into the short hall where I'd left them. Why would she have even thought they were mine?"

Detective McAnally said, "None of the guests in the hotel have registered a Maserati. The Department of Motor Vehicles has no record of a Janet Widlow owning one."

I laughed shakily, weak from the need for food. "Maybe she stole that too." Then quickly, "Forget I said that. I really do need to eat. I just ran four hours on an empty stomach."

"You can go for now, but please stay in town. We may need to talk to you again."

"We're staying over. Hal has a business appointment tomorrow." I returned McAnally's jacket. "Thanks."

Hal was waiting for me outside the door, a can of orange juice and a bagel in his hand. "I made an appointment for a massage for both of us."

"Sounds wonderful." I gulped down the juice and had started on the bagel even before the elevator door opened.

After a hot shower and food, I felt more like myself. I felt even better after the massage. There were gift shops along the corridor to the spa. We walked hand in hand through them before returning to our room. I spotted something in one of the shops that I'd probably buy for Anna before we left.

Hal opened the door to our room, and I stepped inside and froze.

The room had been ransacked. Chair cushions and mattresses had been slit open. Everything had been dumped out of our suitcases. Even Hal's shaving kit had been slashed.

Fear tightened my chest.

"Don't touch anything." Hal was already on his cell phone calling security.

We waited in the upstairs lobby until the police arrived. McAnally and Anderson showed up, and we led them to our room.

"What the hell was in that velvet bag?" I asked, knowing the police must have found it.

They didn't answer, but they exchanged glances that told me I was right about the bag having been found.

"Whatever it was, they think I have it," I said. That frightened me.

The Biltmore wanted to put us up in another wing, on another floor. No charge.

"Not on your life," I said. "Someone here knew our room number, knew I was connected to Janet. Must have guessed she passed that bag to me. We'll stay somewhere else."

"We can't be sure this is connected," McAnally said.

Hal said, "Don't bullshit us. You know it is. Else why didn't they just send a blue suit instead of two Robbery-Homicide detectives?"

Neither detective answered.

Hal used his cell phone to make a reservation at the Bonaventure. An LAPD officer had arrived. To please me, McAnally asked Hal for his car keys and the valet parking ticket, then instructed the officer to retrieve the car and wait for us to pick it up at the nearby Los Angeles Athletic Club. No one would know where we'd be staying.

The only things we could take with us were the clothes we wore. I was glad we had our wallets and IDs.

At the Bonaventure, I changed my looks as best I could by having my hair cut, bleached, and styled. I bought a set of clothes that didn't stand out, but weren't as casual as I usually wear, and I paid for everything in cash.

We spent the rest of the day in our room while I rested from the race. We ordered in and watched movies.

* * *

The next morning, Hal drove to his appointment.

I was convinced now that Janet had deliberately passed the bag to me. It had been a baton pass. We'd both run track and field in college. Your arm goes back, you clamp down hard on the baton, and then you run like hell. She'd been murdered because she didn't have that bag.

She must have discovered someone was after her. I thought she probably ran into the Forecourt to hide or slip away. Only it was a dead end. She was trapped. Her pursuer must have been after that bag, and he must have become enraged when she didn't have it because he risked slashing her throat while all those runners were going by. He'd slipped back here to the Biltmore to ransack our room.

Janet had to have been a drug dealer. A dirty little drug dealer. And what about the phantom Spyder that wasn't registered to a guest or to Janet? Big money bought that car, and she knew its owner. The owner trusted her to drive it. Woman's intuition told me locating the car might be very important—if not to finding her murderer perhaps to uncovering a drug ring. I couldn't think of anything else that would bring in the kind of money required to buy a high end sports car unless she had a millionaire lover. Considering her jealousy over my relationship with Hal, if she'd had such a lover I'm sure she'd have told me. One-upmanship.

My feet were still tender, padded in spots by Dr. Scholl's moleskin, but I was curious enough to want to track down that car. Confident I wouldn't be recognized, I hobbled up to the Biltmore. I needed information and a purchase.

My approach to the valet man about who drove a Maserati was a bust. I don't think the man spoke a word of English.

My main reason for returning to the hotel, however, was to buy a gift for Anna. I searched through the gift shop where I'd seen what I wanted. Finally, the silver locket decorated with light-blue faux gems and zircons I was looking for gleamed at me from a glass case. Perfect for Anna, who had missed the marathon, whose favorite color is blue.

"It's lovely, isn't it?" the shop owner said as she rang it up.

She had graceful hands. Her long acrylic nails were lacquered in red. I watched them as she handled the locket.

"I saw it yesterday. I'm glad it's still here," I said.

Business, she admitted, had been surprisingly slow during the marathon. Part of it had been the wedding reception. "None of those people were interested in faux jewels."

Trolling to see if the Maserati belonged to someone connected to the hotel, I said, "Parking must have been terrible this weekend for the caterers and the people who work in the Biltmore."

"You'd better believe it. We don't often have every bed filled and every ballroom scheduled for an event at once. Same thing today. They're demolishing the parking structure most of us use. Yesterday I had to park a mile away in one of the public lots. It's no better today. Catered luncheons in every ballroom for various conferences. The house is full."

I watched as she pulled a blue velvet bag from underneath the counter and slid Anna's locket into it, and then I stopped breathing.

Ohmygod. Of course. Janet passed the stolen jewels to me. It wasn't drugs at all.

In a trance, I took my package and left the hotel to head for the parking structure she'd told me employees and caterers were using. I was sure I'd find the Maserati there.

I pulled out my cell phone and left a message for Hal. I telephoned Detective McAnally.

"Stay away, Ms. Taylor. Your friend died over those jewels," McAnally said.

"Two other things," I said.

Quickly, I told him about the swarthy busboy who'd threatened Janet and argued with the Mexican waiter. I explained that no one used the staircase. How the tread on Janet's shoes would be those of my New Balances, and if she had used those stairs the morning of the marathon they might learn how she'd come and gone and from which floors. They might even find dust on the shoes of the person who had actually stolen the jewels if that's how they'd slipped up and down.

"What if Janet was in on the heist and then double-crossed the Maserati owner by stealing the jewels? Maybe even took the money. Wouldn't it be helpful to have that car to rule out some of this?" I said.

"Stay away from that parking structure. If we think it's necessary, we'll look into it," McAnally said.

The tone of his voice convinced me I wasn't the only one who thought that car might be important. "I'm only three blocks from there. Think I'll have a look." I hung up smiling. Envisioning a police car roaring in in just a few minutes, I passed the parking structure in question and climbed the hill to the Watercourt.

Like I said, it's a jungle out there, and I am not stupid. I'd already ordered lunch when Hal reached me.

* * *

The Maserati was there, stolen and abandoned, Detective McAnally told us the next morning. In it they'd found the money and the knife used on Janet. The busboy had been Janet's boyfriend. He wasn't a drug dealer, he was an accomplished thief. My friendly Mexican waiter was the fence, and he'd discovered Janet had taken the jewelry.

"Ms. Widlow was no doubt shocked to find her lover, who drove a Maserati, working as a busboy. She hadn't known what he was until she found the stolen jewelry. We think she found it the morning of the marathon and took it with the intention of handing it over to us as soon as she'd finished the race. We doubt she understood the extent of the danger she put herself in.

"When she suspected she was being tailed by her lover, she knew she couldn't risk having the jewels found on her, although she probably didn't know he'd kill her. His fingerprints were on the knife, by the way. Like you, she was an experienced relay competitor. She passed the bag off to you because she thought it was safe. She also knew you'd turn them over to us."

Dismay flooded me. I had so misjudged her! Choosing to dislike her, I'd never made any attempt to find out what was hidden beneath her arrogance. Yet she'd understood me, known I would do the right thing.

"There's a reward for the return of the jewelry. We'll see that you get it."

* * *

We checked out of the hotel an hour later, and bought flowers in the florist shop. Parking near the Chinese Theatre, we walked to the spot where Janet had died, halting in front of a bright mound of flowers, ribbons, candles, and notes. There was a floral arrangement from the theatre owners, but the rest for this impromptu memorial had come from strangers. My heart ached as I leaned to place our flowers with the others.

Hal pointed to a pair of running shoes someone had left. I knelt to read the note attached to them. *For the golden streets of heaven. You go, woman.*

My throat tightened and the ache in my chest enlarged. Through vision blurred by tears, I searched in my purse until I found the narrow red strip for my marathoner's chip, then I picked up one of the shoes and threaded it through the laces. Pressing the Velcro closed, I replaced the shoe.

"Goodbye, friend. Run well," I whispered. "Beat us all."

A blood-red sunset paints the sky over southeast Los Angeles. Along Slauson Avenue, the traffic's roar echoes off hard-edged factories and warehouses. We have arrived at a crossroad in time, to the site of an infamous landmark that progress has swept away. If you close your eyes and listen, soon you'll hear it. The sweet notes of a jazz trumpet playing a tune that blared out of every jukebox in Los Angeles.

The song is "Sleepy Lagoon" and the date is August 2, 1942. Open your eyes. The factories are gone and you're standing by the edge of an urban reservoir nicknamed **Sleepy Lagoon**, *a popular swimming hole for the local Mexican-Americans denied access to the public pools. In the summer of 1942, the tranquil setting forever changed when the body of José Diaz was discovered there. The events that followed – the mass hysteria, a bigoted press, and corrupt trial became one of LA's darkest chapters and sparked the Zoot Suit Riots of '43. Even today, one can only speculate what other dark secrets lie buried at Sleepy Lagoon.*

Or can we?

SLEEPY LAGOON NOCTURNE
by Paul D. Marks

Hot jazz—swing music—boogied, bopped and jived. And Bobby Saxon was one of those who made it happen. Bobby banged the eighty-eights with the Booker "Boom-Boom" Taylor Orchestra in the Club Alabam down on Central Avenue. It was the heppest place for whites to come slumming and mix with the coloreds. That's just the way it was in those days, Los Angeles in the 1940s during the war.

Bobby was the only white musician in an otherwise all-colored orchestra. But that didn't really make him feel like an outsider. He came in to the Alabam early almost every day to practice. His apartment was too small for a piano and, besides, the landlord wouldn't abide the noise.

"Where's Gaby been?" Bobby shouted across the empty club to Lawrence, the Alabam's chief bartender, who was setting up the bar. Lawrence shrugged, the smoke from his Pall Mall drifting aimlessly across the room. The club always seemed a little strange to Bobby in the daytime. There were no windows, and with the house lights turned on some of the mystery seeped out.

Bobby flipped his chocolate brown fedora onto the top of the piano, slicked back his dark hair, and wondered about what might have happened to Gaby, the janitor. He hadn't shown up in at least a couple of weeks.

* * *

Tim Naylor let the music wash over him. "Sleepy Lagoon" flowed from the RCA radio, a languid song filled with yearning. The song conjured up a certain mood for Tim. He wished he had a special girl to share it with. And he tried not to think about what the words *sleepy lagoon* had come to mean lately—a murder, a trial and the Zoot Suit Riots.

The song ended and the announcer came on with the latest war news. The Marines were trying to take the island of Peleliu, losing as many men, maybe more, to malaria as to the Japanese. On the other side of the world, American and British troops tried to reach a bridge too far. And all the time Tim was trying to keep in mind what FDR had said, that the only thing to fear is fear itself.

Tim worked at The Darkroom on Wilshire Boulevard, a camera shop that looked like a camera—you entered through the lens—mostly in the back, developing photos. Sometimes up front with the customers. He fanned the pictures from two rolls of film he had developed a couple weeks ago out on the counter in front of him and stared at them longer than he should have. He hoped his boss, Mr. Daniels, wouldn't see. The first roll were photos of a Mexican fiesta, lots of food and children banging away at a *piñata*. The second roll intrigued him more. Glamour shots of a beautiful woman with an enigmatic smile on her lips, not unlike the Mona Lisa's. There were shots of her in trousers and shadow, like a silver and black Marlene Dietrich publicity still, that made her even more appealing. In others she wore a long veil and little else and looked coyly away from the prying camera. Tim was sure she was the most beautiful woman he'd ever seen. If for no other reason, he wanted to find Gaby Rodriguez, the fellow who'd brought the film in, so he could ask about the woman in the photos. These shots were as good as anything Hurrell had done. Highly stylized, dramatic. Sensual. Tim, always with a Brownie camera at the ready, wished he'd taken the pictures. Perhaps he could, some day.

"Tim," Harvey Daniels shouted toward the back room, "stop staring at those photos and get out here."

Tim took one last look at the pictures, set them down and darted out of the back room, wiping his hands on his apron. At nineteen, he had already enlisted in the Marines. He wanted to go fight the Germans or Japanese, like everyone else. College could wait. Marriage could wait. Everything but the Marines could wait. It was only a couple weeks till he was off to boot camp. He was gung ho to be a combat photographer, but a rifleman would be just as good. And more than anything he hoped he'd get in before the war ended.

"I know what you been doing," Mr. Daniels said. "Lookin' at those pictures again. Well, see if you can find *Señor* Rodriguez. I don't want to eat the cost of the prints and developing. Hell, it's been two weeks."

Normally Mr. Daniels wouldn't have been so anxious after only two weeks. But he didn't trust *pachucos*—which for him included anyone of Mexican heritage—and wanted to make sure he wouldn't get stiffed.

Tim dialed the number on Mr. Rodriguez's envelope. It rang seventeen times. No answer. He tried several more times over the next few days. There was still no answer, so he headed over to the address in East Hollywood, on his own time.

The address on the envelope was for a small

courtyard apartment. Palm trees dotted the front lawn and tropical plants filled the planters. Just like most of the people in Los Angeles, little here was native to the L.A. basin. Tim pressed the doorbell and waited. His finger ran over the envelopes of pictures. Curiosity may have killed the cat; Tim hoped it wouldn't kill him as he opened the envelope and pulled the photos out, staring again at the lovely woman.

No one was home. He figured he'd try the work address on the envelope tomorrow.

* * *

Bobby sat at the piano and did some practice runs. His long, slender fingers ran over the keyboard, nimble gazelles. He worked over "La Tempesta," one of the band's signature songs and one that featured Bobby on the piano. But he drifted from the fury of that to the sensuality of "Sleepy Lagoon," a song made famous by big band leader Harry James. Sleepy Lagoon had been famous in Los Angeles during the war years, not the song but the place – a lover's lane for the Mexican kids on the East side of L.A. Just the title brought up images of palm trees, tranquil azure waters, lovers in each other's arms. But today it brought pictures of murder and Mexican-American kids being hauled off to jail, a long trial and appeals. The Sleepy Lagoon murder case was the spark that some said led to the Zoot Suit Riots, though Bobby thought it was more complicated than that. Despite that, the song still requested a lot. And Bobby liked it.

Booker sauntered in like he owned the joint, smoke drifting up from the ever-present Lucky Strike in an ebony holder. Wherever Booker went, he acted like he owned the joint. And he wouldn't take any guff off white folks, not even white cops. Bobby'd heard that Booker had killed a man once. Booker neither confirmed nor denied it. "Good for the reputation," was all he'd say. Bobby left it at that. He wasn't sure he wanted to know the truth.

"Bobby, my man," Booker said, heading for the piano. "Let's take it out back."Bobby knew what that meant. He followed Booker through the eerie emptiness to the alley behind the club. Booker was already reaching into his pocket, coming out with a fat reefer and a solid gold lighter. He snuffed out the Lucky Strike, put the holder in his pocket and lit up the reefer. The Booker "Boom Boom" Taylor Orchestra—really a big band and not an orchestra in the classical sense—had seen its share of success, though nothing to compare with Miller, Goodman, Ellington. Whatever success they'd had, Bobby couldn't see how it could afford Booker a solid gold lighter. Another mystery—another clue to his past?

Booker passed the jive stick over to Bobby, who took a long drag. They passed it back and forth a couple times. With each hit Bobby felt more reflective. He wondered about his future. What would he be doing in ten years? Still playing juke joints? Would he ever find someone to love? Would the war intervene? He didn't want to think about it and besides, it was hard to think about it in the haze of marijuana smoke. He didn't really like smoking, but in order to be one of the boys he figured he had to.

"I think the powers that be are talking about finding a replacement for your pal Gaby."

"You have some sway with them, Booker. Can you ask them to hold off? I'm sure he'll be back."

"I know you're tight with him. I'll see what I can do."
Booker took an extra long drag. "The boys should be getting
here by now. Let's go jam it up a little. Got a new number I
want to try out."

When Bobby and Booker returned to the murky
daytime dusk of the club, Bobby half expected to see Gaby
there with his mop and bucket, as usual. Adjusting his eyes
from the bright sun outside, Bobby saw that Lawrence was
no longer alone. But there was no Gaby. Instead, there was
a gangly young man who Lawrence introduced as Tim
Naylor. A good looking kid who reminded Bobby of a taller,
lankier version of Alan Ladd. Tim explained about Mr.
Rodriguez's photos that hadn't been picked up at the camera
store where he worked. That piqued Bobby's interest. He
knew what a photo bug Gaby was. He would never leave
pictures languishing. His dream was to one day set up a
photo lab in his apartment, if he could ever afford one with
a second bathroom, and take pictures for *Life* magazine.

Bobby asked to see the pictures. Booker had better
things to do and took a powder as Tommy handed them
over. Bobby scanned the two rolls, one with photos of a
woman who seemed as if she was hiding something, the
other with pictures of a Mexican fiesta. At the end of the
fiesta roll were two pictures that didn't seem to belong. An
empty field. At the back of the photo of the field was a car.
He wondered if it was Gaby's car, but the color didn't look
right and it was very small in the frame. The other odd
photo was of a Mexican market. Bobby didn't notice
anything else unusual about them and slipped them back in
the pack. Maybe Gaby had just run off a couple of random
shots to finish up the roll of film.

"Do you mind if I keep these for a few days?" Bobby

said.

"I don't think I should. Boss wouldn't like it."

"Bobby knew Gaby pretty well," Lawrence said. "They's buddies." He lit a new Pall Mall off the one in his mouth.

Bobby offered to pay for the film.

"I figure all Mr. Daniels wants is his money, so I guess you can have them." Tim took the bills from Bobby. He hesitated before handing over the pictures.

"What is it?" Bobby said.

"Do you mind if I keep one picture?"

Bobby wasn't sure what he was getting at. Tim looked through the photos of the woman. He pulled one photo from the set. Half of the woman's pearl white face stood out from the dark background. The other half was shrouded in mystery and blackness. A peek-a-boo wave descended over one eye, à la Veronica Lake. Her eyes sparkled. And her mouth turned up in the slightest way, suggesting that maybe she knew something you didn't, but that you wished you did.

"She's a dish," Tim said, handing the packets of pictures to Bobby, "I know it's crazy, but I think I'm in love with her. I can't get her out of my mind."

What could Bobby do now? He didn't want to leave the picture with Tim, but to take it back forcefully would create too much of a scene. He let the boy keep the picture. Tim rabbited after that.

Bobby sat down at the piano, spread the pictures out on top of it. One roll to his left, the other to his right. In between them was a highball—Bobby's drink of choice—that Lawrence had set there. Bobby could feel Lawrence standing over his shoulder, admiring the pictures,

particularly those of the alluring woman. Even with the
house lights up full, it was still dim in the club, adding to
the woman's mysterious aura.

"Such a fine specimen of a woman." Lawrence nudged
Bobby's shoulder. "But looks to me like she's hiding
something."

"It's just the low key lighting," Bobby said. He
shuffled the pictures of the woman back into a stack, then
did the same with the fiesta pictures. He put the fiesta
shots in his left pocket, the mystery woman in his right.

He had known Gaby for almost a year now, ever since
Gaby had come to work at the Alabam. They had taken to
each other. Both felt a little like outsiders in the colored
club. But Bobby felt at home with Gaby. There was just
something about him. Gaby, in his forties, had acted almost
like a father to the much younger Bobby from the start. He
had seen things about Bobby that no one else had.

More activity now as the band started filtering in.
Instruments came out. Booker brought out his new chart.
Everyone blew hard.

A few hours later the club was filled to overflowing.
Bobby and the band cranked out a raging version of "La
Tempesta" that got the whole joint wailing. Some whites
and coloreds were even dancing with each other. The Club
Alabam was just about the only place in L.A. you could do
that and get away with your life. And it was just about the
only place Bobby could be himself.

Music was Bobby's life—what he lived for. The
sacrifices he'd made to be a musician. But right now, he
wasn't thinking about the music. It just came from
somewhere inside him.

Where the hell was Gaby?

* * *

The next evening, Bobby rang the doorbell to Gaby's East Hollywood apartment. He knew that Serita, Gaby's wife, worked two jobs to help make ends meet. He looked to the wall across the courtyard, a picture of Kilroy painted there with the words *"Kilroy estaba aquí"* under it. This little man seemed to be everywhere these days, from the front lines in Europe to the walls of Hollywood. Kilroy was everywhere, even in Spanish.

Serita opened the door, recognized Bobby and invited him in. Offered him a *cervesa*. It was obvious Serita had been crying, though she tried not to show it as she sat under a large, hand-painted crucifix. Bobby asked where Gaby was. Serita didn't know. She was afraid to go to the police because they didn't care about Mexicans.

"Look what happened at Sleepy Lagoon," she said.

Bobby had read about Sleepy Lagoon in the papers. It had been front page news for some time now. The lagoon was a reservoir used for watering crops on a ranch in East L.A. By day it was also a swimming hole for Mexican kids who couldn't use the public pools. By night it was a lover's lane. A Mexican-American boy had been killed and the police had rounded up more than three hundred Mexican-American youths in a dragnet. Twenty-three of them were eventually charged with murder. Several were convicted. Shortly after the convictions, L.A. erupted into the Zoot Suit Riots. Sailors and soldiers going after Mexican boys dressed in the baggy-pantsed suits. The city was high on adrenalin and everyone was scared. The servicemen stripped the zoot suits from the boys and burned them in the streets. The *pachucos* fought back.

Bobby had no idea what that might have to do with

Gaby and his pictures, other than Serita's fear that the police wouldn't care about a missing Mexican.

There was nothing in the Rodriguez apartment to say that this wasn't the all-American family. A picture of FDR hung near a bookshelf, a small American flag waved from a stand nearby. Inexpensive landscapes and Norman Rockwell prints filled the walls. The rest of the walls were filled with Gaby's photos, large prints, small prints, buildings, faces.

"He thought he'd taken the picture that would make him. He was very excited." But Serita hadn't seen the picture, didn't know what it was. She poured a beer into a glass for Bobby. "He thought it would get him into *Life* magazine."

Bobby pulled out the photos from his left hand pocket. The fiesta roll. He didn't think Serita needed to see the other roll, at least not yet. Besides, he already knew who the woman was and where the photos had been taken. He didn't know if the pictures on either roll had anything to do with Gaby's disappearance, but it was worth a shot. He explained how he had come by them.

Serita looked at the pictures. "These couldn't be what he was talking about. There's nothing *sensacional* here."

"Where were these taken?"

Serita glanced at the photos. "My cousin's eighth birthday party."

"In East L.A.?"

"*Si*, yes," Serita said.

"What about these?" Bobby sipped his beer, slid the last two shots on the roll—the vacant field and the Mexican market – across the table to Serita. She brushed her sleek, black hair away from her eyes as she examined them.

She looked at them again. "I don't know, maybe over by Sleepy Lagoon."

"What makes you say that?"

"My cousins live near there. And see this *carniceria* on the corner." She pointed to the mom and pop market in the photo. "And this group of palm trees. Of course they could have a *carniceria* anywhere, but not that group of trees."

Serita held onto the photos as if they could bring Gaby back. Bobby asked her for them, explaining he needed them to help track down Gaby. She reluctantly handed them to him.

They talked a few more minutes, then Bobby left. He wanted to drive by the field in the photo, but didn't have time. Maybe tomorrow. He had to get to work at the Alabam.

* * *

Tim sat in his parents' kitchen after they'd gone to bed, staring at the picture of the mystery woman. He felt stupid for not making dupes of the photos before he gave them to that musician, negs and all. He felt silly falling in love with a picture, someone he knew nothing about. Still, there was something that drew him to her. Enigmatic in the half light. He had no steady girl and maybe he just needed someone to latch onto before heading off to the Marines.

* * *

The next morning Bobby got up early and drove down Slauson, toward Sleepy Lagoon. He didn't know what else to do, figured it was better than doing nothing. The area was only partially developed. A lot of open space. The old L.A. breathed here—*El Pueblo de Nuestra Señora la Reina de los Angeles de Porciúncula.* On the way to the Lagoon, Bobby passed the *carniceria* in the picture. He stopped, took the pictures out, examined them. This was definitely the market in the photo.

He drove on down the road toward the lagoon, got out of the car and looked around. Everything seemed the same as in the pictures except for the car at the right hand side of the photo, which wasn't there now. Date palms swayed in the morning breeze. It was early, not many people about except for a couple of old women heading to the market, dragging their shopping carts behind them. Bobby's skin crawled with the grit of the Santa Ana winds; he scratched, but it didn't do any good. He walked to his Studebaker and drove off. There was nothing to see right now so Bobby headed back to more familiar territory.

He found Tim on the street, snapping pictures of the low rise Wilshire skyline, and just about ready to open up The Darkroom for the day.

"Did you find what happened to your friend, Mr. Rodriquez?" Tim said.

Bobby shook his head.

"Or who that girl is?"

Bobby ignored that, said, "Can you blow up a couple pictures for me, or at least a section of them? I'd like to see the car in the photo better. Closer."

"Sure. Before the boss gets in."

Bobby handed him the negatives for the fiesta roll, asking him to blow up the last two pictures on the roll.

Tim jammed into The Darkroom in back. He tried to block Bobby from entering. Was he trying to hide something? Bobby pushed his way past Tim into the little room. The acrid smell of developing chemicals burned his nostrils. He looked up to see a huge blowup of the mystery woman that Tim had obviously made from the photo Bobby had let him keep.

Tim blushed like a little boy: "I made the blowup from the print you let me keep. It's not as good as having the negative, but better than nothing. Hey, I can't help it. I'm in love."

"You never met her."

"Doesn't matter. There's something about her. Like in that movie *Laura*, where the detective, Dana Andrews, falls in love with Laura's picture. Why should I be different?"

"That's a movie."

"And this is Hollywood. What's the difference?"

Bobby didn't have an argument for that.

Tim did what he had to do with the negatives. Bobby watched, though his attention kept returning to the blowup of the woman.

When the job was done, Tim handed Bobby the blowups he'd made from the two photos on the fiesta roll. Bobby could make out all the letters on the license plate of the car, frame right. He handed Tim a ten dollar bill for a two dollar job, told him to keep the change. He took the blowups and scrammed out of there.

Bobby wanted someone to run the plates on the car in the photo blowup. And Booker was the kind of man who always knew someone who knew someone who could get you pretty much anything you wanted. But hell, it was barely noon. Way too early for Booker to be awake. He could chance going by Booker's house, but why get him p.o.'d before even asking for the favor? He drove home, thinking he might get some more sleep.

* * *

Bobby threw his hat on the table, crashed on the living room couch. His bones ached. He hoped for sleep. He could usually sleep pretty well during the day. Not today. He lay there, staring at the cracks in the plaster ceiling. He thought about enlisting, fighting Hitler and Hirohito, but knew it would never happen—he'd never pass the physical. He reached inside his pockets, pulling out both packets of pictures. He set the fiesta roll aside and gazed at the mystery woman on the other roll—Tim's dream lover.

But she wasn't such a mystery to Bobby. He took the pictures of her and locked them in his lower desk drawer. He left the other packet of pictures out on the coffee table.

Sleep was impossible. He listened to news of the war on the radio, until it was time to go try Booker.

* * *

Bobby had brought the pictures over to Booker's house in the afternoon. By that evening's gig at the Alabam he had the information. He pulled Bobby aside, puffing on a Lucky Strike in the sleek, ebony holder.

"Bobby, my man," Booker said. "I don't know what you want this info for, but I don't think you gonna like the results."

"Shoot," Bobby said.

"That car, it belongs to the police. LAPD's what I'm talkin' 'bout." Booker ran his long, sculpted fingers through his marcelled hair.

That put a whole new spin on Gaby, his pictures and his disappearance. After the Sleepy Lagoon mess, why would he be taking pictures of Sleepy Lagoon with an unmarked police car in the background? Why would an unmarked police car be there? Why was Gaby missing?

Bobby headed to the alley for some air. Saw a freshly painted "Kilroy Was Here" on the wall. It hadn't been there the other night when he and Booker were outside smoking reefer. But these days Kilroy was everywhere.

A man in a double-breasted suit with his hat pulled low over his eyes followed Bobby out.

"Got a butt?" the man said.

Bobby shook his head. The man pulled out his own pack of Camels, lit up without offering Bobby one. Which was just as well with him. He smoked with Booker and the band to be one of the boys. He didn't feel like he had to to buddy up with a customer. Although this guy didn't look like the club's typical customer. He was as large as a Frigidaire and definitely looked like rough trade from the wrong side of the tracks. He sidled up to Bobby, inhaled deeply on his cigarette and let it out.

"A word to the wise, bud. Lay off."

"What're you talking about?"

The man leaned into Bobby, forcing his back against the cold club wall. "I think you know. Cameras, missing wetbacks. It's unhealthy." The man sucked on his cigarette and split. Bobby watched him walk up the alley, waited until he was gone and then headed back into the club.

Bobby wasn't sure how to interpret what just happened. The one thing he knew for sure was that he was on the right track. Something had happened to Gaby and someone didn't want him following up on it. That only made him more determined. But what if the guy was a cop or a gangster? And which was worse? What would either want with Gaby? And how did they come on Bobby? From Booker running the plates—someone must have tipped them off.

* * *

Bobby spent the rest of the night after the gig in his apartment staring at the two pictures from the end of the fiesta roll. He was getting a bad feeling about Gaby now. He didn't think his friend was just missing anymore, on a lark with another woman. Or on a bender. Gaby had seen something, had photographed it. And now he was missing. But Bobby still couldn't tell what Gaby might have stumbled across in the photos.

He went into the small green and white tiled bathroom, running his eyes over the little Egyptian pyramids the tile made, until he came to the mirror. His eyes looked red, puffy. Tired. Why not, he'd only gotten a couple hours' sleep. He whipped off his coat and tie, setting them on the tub. Then his shirt. He stared at his reflection. The close-cropped dark hair, smooth skin, chin too weak for a man. His eyes settled on his chest and the small, round breasts—and he was no longer Bobby, but Roberta.

Bobby had been born Roberta and still was, at least underneath the double-breasted pin-stripe suits and Dick Tracy hats. But in order to pursue her dream of being a musician in a hot jazz band, she had to pretend to be a man. The ruse worked. Nobody suspected. Or if they did, no one said anything...until Gaby had come to work at the Alabam. He sensed something was amiss about Bobby from the beginning. He saw something in Bobby that didn't seem to fit the hard-edged musician, and Bobby finally admitted the truth to him. Bobby tried to avoid him at first. He didn't want his secret to come out. They were both outsiders, trying to pass in worlds that weren't really theirs. It actually made a bond between them, and their friendship grew from there. It grew to the point that Gaby had talked Bobby—Roberta—into posing for some pictures. Letting her feminine side show. A side she had to keep hidden most of the time. She didn't like the idea, but Gaby convinced her he needed some glamour shots for his portfolio. The more he talked of it, the more it grew on her. She was only glad that the pictures and negatives had fallen into her hands—all except for one. She wouldn't let the others go and if Tim ever asked about them she'd say she'd lost them.

Staring in the mirror, she watched herself, wondering what it might be like to live as a woman once more.

Bobby threw on a robe, went back to the living room. She stared at the photos again – there had to be something there. She held a magnifying glass over the first picture, then the other. Back and forth. There was a dark shape in the middle of the second photo. She couldn't quite tell what it was. A couple people maybe? Hard to say. She'd have to have Tim blow the pictures up again, larger, the whole frame, not just the license plate on the car.

A crimson knife edge of light was just slicing over the horizon, seeping in through the windows. The walls of Bobby's apartment closed in on her. She would have crawled up them if she could have. She dressed in her suit and tie, grabbed the photos and her hat, headed to the Studebaker and then The Darkroom. Though the city was rising, it was too early for Tim or almost anyone to be at work. Bobby paced. Wilshire Boulevard was deserted except for a swarm of cars heading downtown from West Los Angeles. Bobby eyed them suspiciously. He felt as if he was being followed. Had he seen too many crime movies?

* * *

Tim showed a few minutes before nine. Bobby had almost worn a hole in his wingtips from all his pacing. They went into the store. Tim did his magic on the negatives again.

Bobby had been right. Two men in suits and hats at the back of the field. The picture was fuzzy, having been blown up so large, but it looked like they were holding bats—billy clubs?—high in the air, as they pounded a third man on the ground. Cops? Was the man on the ground a belated Sleepy Lagooner getting his? Did Gaby capture more on film than was good for his health? Bobby stared at the men in the photo. One of them might have been the guy who braced him in the alley. He couldn't see the man's face in the blurry photo, but he had the same Frigidaire build. Bobby blasted out of there like a torpedo escaping a submarine. He dashed to his Studebaker, tires squealing away from the curb. He didn't really need the speed, but his blood was pumping. In the rearview mirror, he saw Tim standing on the curb staring after him

The Studebaker tooled down Wilshire. Bobby's mind wasn't on his driving. He wanted to know what the hell had happened to Gaby. He didn't know where else to go, but Sleepy Lagoon.

Bobby made it there in record time. He walked the field leading to the lagoon, bending every now and then to examine something in the weeds, maybe pick something up.

He figured he might find something that would tell him about Gaby's disappearance.

He spotted a pile of leaves that seemed out of place. Toed it with his shoe. Something glinted under the surface. He pushed the leaves aside with his hands, retrieved a Leica camera—just like Gaby's. The lens was cracked, the film missing. But he knew it was Gaby's by the braided strap. And he knew the worst had happened.

"Jesus," he whispered, as if someone might be there to hear. Or maybe it was wishful thinking. Then he heard the sound, a screech, as if from a dying animal. He slid to the ground, then looked up to see where the sound was coming from. Two men in suits had a third on the ground, whaling away at him with nightsticks. Bobby wasn't sure what to do. He wanted to save the man on the ground, but he had no weapon and he was no physical match for the two large men in suits and Dick Tracy hats, who looked like cops straight from Central Casting. Straight out of the photos he'd had Tim blow up for him that morning.

Bobby ran toward the men. They were so intent on the job at hand they didn't hear his panting or the rustling of the dry grass. Bobby didn't know what he'd do when he got to them, but maybe he could make it stop.

He knew he couldn't beat them in a fight, fair or otherwise. They were huge, they were tough, they had billy clubs, and if they were indeed cops, guns. And they damn well looked like cops. But he wouldn't back down. He planted his feet, ready for whatever might come. He had to do this, for Gaby. For himself.

The larger man—the one from the alley—looked up, briskly walked straight toward Bobby. The other man, not as large, grabbed his partner's arm. Bobby waited.

The men stopped, frozen like deer in headlights.

After a moment, the men surprised him by turning and heading to their car, which was parked on the far side of the lagoon. Bobby couldn't figure out why they had retreated. Maybe they were confident enough to know nothing would happen to them. So why complicate things by killing a white musician?

He heard a noise behind him—someone running lickety split. He turned to see Tim jogging toward him, Brownie in hand, furiously snapping pictures. Behind Tim stood the cabbie who had brought him. Maybe there were just too many witnesses.

Any way you looked at it, Bobby was happy to see those men heading the other way and Tim's grinning face.

* * *

Gaby's body was found buried on the far side of the lagoon, along with two others that were never identified. Everyone figured this is where the bad cops took people for private "punishment." Gaby's crime: he had photographed them in the act of punishing someone else – the someone in the photo blowups. That was enough to sign his own death warrant. And now everyone knew they did it. Some cared. Some didn't. Bobby having Booker check the plate had tipped the cops to him. But they figured the visit to Bobby at the club would have scared him off. They never expected Bobby to come snooping around their stomping grounds.

To no one's surprise, the cops got off with a slap on the wrist. A week later, the paper said two detectives were fired from the department for insubordination. They would receive their pensions. Bobby could picture them under a palm tree by some tranquil water, not unlike the languorous "Sleepy Lagoon," a torch song playing, with a rum and Coca-Cola in their hands, just like in the song. Yeah, it would be a rough life for them.

* * *

Bobby held Serita's hand at Gaby's funeral. She was surrounded by family, but took Bobby a few yards away, off by themselves, under a large oak tree.

"He liked you, Bobby. He told me so. Said you were special." She wiped her eyes with a handkerchief. "He thought of you as a friend, not just someone who worked with him. And now, now you've found him and his killers. You are *un buen compadre.*"

"I'm only sorry they're not going to San Quentin." Bobby squeezed Serita's hand. He thought about the boy the two Central Casting cops were beating the day he'd gone to the lagoon. He'd survived, unlike Gaby and the two unidentified bodies. He went back to Mexico to live with his family.

Bobby knew Serita missed Gaby. There would be a hole in her life for a long time to come. He missed Gaby too. He could be himself around Gaby and thought Gaby felt the same. He couldn't cry now. He was a man. But when he got home later he knew the tears would come.

Serita broke away from Bobby to join her family. Tim made his way over to Bobby. "I'm sorry about your friend."

"He was a good guy," Bobby said. "And how the hell did you wind up at Sleepy Lagoon that day? Not that I was unhappy to see you."

"I knew something was wrong the way you ran out of

The Darkroom. Figured you might need some help. Besides, you're my only link to the woman in the picture." Tim had a faraway look in his eye. "You know her, don't you? The woman in the pictures?"

Bobby didn't respond. Finally, he said, "What're you looking for, Tim? You look like you're a million miles away."

"I guess I am. I know it sounds silly, my heart is thinking of her, but my mind is looking to the Pacific. I suppose I'll be there soon—I'm leaving for boot camp next week." He saluted playfully. "I'd like to meet her some time. I'd be a perfect gentleman."

"I'm sure you would be," Bobby said. "Maybe I'll introduce you to her one day."

* * *

"Sleepy Lagoon" ended and the Woolworth's juke went on to another song. Bobby looked up, waking from his dream world, back in the present. No more war. No more Sleepy Lagoons. He reached into his pocket and put a couple bucks on the counter. He knew it was way too much. It was for "Sleepy Lagoon" on the jukebox and his friend Gaby. He headed for the front door, past the photo counter, where all the new Kodaks were on display, and thought of Tim. Would he ever have introduced Tim to the woman in the pictures? He didn't know, but it was an intriguing idea.

He thought about Gaby and Tim, the Zoot Suit Riots and Sleepy Lagoon. The appeals court had overturned the verdict and the Mexican boys had been set free—seemed like the cops just wanted to pin it on someone Mexican and it didn't matter if it was the right Mexican. And no one knew who killed the boy that sparked the whole thing in the first place.

Bobby walked up the street, past a faded "Kilroy was here." Since the war that little guy wasn't as popular.

Perhaps Tim and Bobby could have been friends, but Tim joined the service not long after the incident at Sleepy Lagoon and was killed on Okinawa, the last battle of the war. He was found with a Brownie camera and a picture of a mysterious brunette in his possession. Nobody knew who she was or how to inform her of his death.

And that's just the way it was in those days.

The California Institute of Technology, (Caltech) is as much a place of scientific discovery as it is a seat of higher learning. Situated in history-rich Pasadena, Caltech is an elite think tank for the brainy bunch, drawing to its campus research scientists, mathematicians, geophysicists, astrophysicists, chemists, biologists, psycho biologists . . . the list of goes on, and that's not counting the Nobel Prize winners. There have been at least thirty, including Albert Einstein and Richard Feynman. Numerous scientific milestones are attributed to this landmark Institute . . . the discovery of anti-matter, the birth of modern earthquake study, the dawn of aerospace, left brain/right brain functions to name a few. The Jet Propulsion Lab is part of Caltech. So is the Seismological Laboratory that tracks California's earthquakes. It's clear that the best and the brightest minds gravitate here, but occasionally, the wicked and the depraved prowl the wide walkways, ready to pounce on their unsuspecting prey . . .

IT DOESN'T TAKE A GENIUS
by Kate Thornton

"Miss Dean, it doesn't take a genius to get these billings right," Dr. Buehring said in that annoying nasal sneer of his, tossing the file folders on my desk without a second glance at me.

You'd think having a job at Caltech would make me smart, but that's not how it works. There are plenty of regular people working here, average folks like you and me who do average jobs in departments like Finance and Administration. Sure, we all get to see people like Stephen Hawking and Kip Thorne once in a while—after all, it *is* the California Institute of Technology—but only the students and the faculty are really smart. Everyone else is practically invisible.

Caltech is a beautiful place with wide walkways and flower plantings everywhere. Only blocks from Pasadena's best shopping district, it is an eclectic assortment of buildings, including Beckman Auditorium, a birthday-cake of a round theater, and a library that looks like a savings and loan. The faculty club is called the Athenaeum, and everyone says it looks like a European museum. I have never been in it, so I don't know. I don't eat with the Nobel Prize winners.

The Business Administration building is a

nondescript box across the street from the main campus, but when the new computer systems were installed for payroll and accounting, we all had to learn the new programs. Most of us in the Finance Department were already pretty much up to speed, but the Institute got a great group rate on the training, and since everyone in Dr. Buehring's office figured three days in a computer class was better than working, we all signed up. I was in a class of fifteen people, most of whom I knew through casual conversations at the water cooler. The class was divided about evenly between men and women, but I was the oldest woman there. Okay, I was the oldest person there.

When I think back on it, I wonder that no one ever noticed me. But try being a middle-aged, slightly overweight woman at a place like Caltech—or anywhere, I guess—and you'll know what invisibility really means.

The other women in the class were a cliquish bunch of chattering young things who talked mostly about television, movie stars, their hair and their social lives.

The men were familiar, too. Five of them were guys from my own department who understood the value of getting a training ticket punched, regular guys who worked the dull jobs and hoped for management promotions.

It was the other two who caught my attention.

They both worked in our Shipping and Receiving area, entirely different from the shirt and tie guys in Finance and totally unlike the unkempt but brilliant students their age.

Brian Spain was big, almost hulking, with his hair shorn so close it reminded me of a convict cut. Funny how fashions do a one-eighty every so often—the way kids dress these days would have been laughed at twenty years ago.

He had that fast-food beefiness and kept a soda in his meaty paw. He prided himself on being a shoot-'em-up video game whiz, but looked like he might be pretty slow on his feet in any kind of a real situation. Tony Brandt was different. Tony was small and wiry, with that same ugly haircut, and a pitiful growth of fuzz at the very end of his chin. He had sharp features and a manic manner, and like Brian, was some sort of video game aficionado. Only he looked as if he might actually be fast enough on his feet to do something more than just brag.

I guess I wouldn't have noticed them if I had not overheard them talking about the instructor, Jennifer Pearson, at lunch. She was a pretty young thing, twenty-something and very energetic. She seemed bright, too, but it wasn't her brains they were discussing.

I hadn't intended to follow them—I just wanted to wander around the campus and find a little something to eat that wasn't either coated in sugar or deep fried or both. I went to the student food court and found a salad and a table near a large fake palm. They were parked at a table on the other side of it, gorging on burritos.

"Yeah, well, I could take her easy," Tony was saying between mouthfuls.

"You think," Brian said. "She'd be a handful, though, wouldn't she?"

"There'd be more than enough for both of us," Tony said, "I say we go for it."

"You go for it, Tony. I'll just watch. Besides, what are you gonna do, ask her out?" Brian's speech was a little slow as he crammed down more burrito.

Tony laughed. "Yeah, like she'd go out with me. Hey, I don't even bother asking them out anymore. The stupid bitches, I just pick one and make a plan."

They were speaking in low tones, so I leaned in a little more closely. It was the sort of moronic chat that could make me sick, but I listened with morbid fascination.

"So what's your plan with this one?"

"Miss Know-it-all Fuckin' Pearson? Hah, she's gonna be surprised. Tonight I just do a little recon, then tomorrow I set the plan. Wednesday I take her, and then, hey, we'll be out of the class and no one will be the wiser. The pictures will be up and the money will flow."

"So, like, they never remember what you do to 'em? How can they not remember?"

"The stuff is like, fuckin' awesome, Bri. They never see it coming, you can do what you want to them and they don't remember when it's over. The only time you have to be careful is when you're getting it in their drinks."

"Shit, man, tell me again about that girl from Occidental last month, the one you messed up." I heard the edge in his voice, a breathless catch.

Tony began a rambling story about a girl he had drugged and raped, and then—just for the fun of it—cut up with an Exacto knife. My skin crawled as I remembered the news story about her. She was a nineteen-year-old journalism major from Eagle Rock who couldn't remember anything after going to the campus cafeteria for a Coke one evening. She had awakened in her car, in a sticky pool of blood that had oozed from the patterns on her face and body. She was still hospitalized in a psychiatric ward.

My stomach lurched, but I continued to listen.

"Hey, I got her pictures up on the website already," Tony said. "Only the select few can see them, though."

"Yeah, cool the way it's protected," Brian said. "You

could put up anything on the Internet and never get caught. So, like, how do you get the money?"

Tony explained that just as a cryptic password was needed to view his pornographic website of horrors, he had an elaborate method of collecting credit card payments from the subscribers. "It's too cool, Dude, the website pays for the drugs and I get digital pictures of everything. Just wait until next week when the computer class bitch is up on the site. She's gonna be number four, but the best one yet. I think my mistake with that college bitch was letting her live. This one's gonna be so fuckin' messed up she'll never talk about it. The sickos are gonna pay real big for a snuffer. Hey, a picture's worth a thousand fuckin' words anyway, huh?" Tony laughed.

I wanted to tell Jennifer Pearson, warn her. Even though I didn't know her and could barely imagine approaching her with this kind of lurid tale, I knew I had to do something. I decided to tell Jennifer as soon as an opportunity presented itself, even if it meant embarrassment and awkwardness. I thought about going to the police, but that was out of the question. I had cried wolf too often, and the local cops knew me as a busybody, a middle-aged lonely woman who complained too much about her noisy neighbors. I just didn't want to deal with them, and I knew they didn't want to deal with me.

What I really wanted was to get to that website and prove it belonged to Tony Brandt, but without the password I knew I'd never find it. It would have been great to know a Computer Science major, but I didn't know anyone at Caltech except other people like me. The students were like another species, and the faculty was unapproachable.

I listened to them talk a bit more, but all I learned

was that they were both going to follow Jennifer after work that afternoon. I made plans to do the same.

Later in class, I hit the Internet instead of doing the exercises. I searched on the date rape drug for starters and came up with Rohypnol, or "roofies." I searched the seamier websites, too, cruising for the kind of sadism that might attract a similar audience to Tony's. I was about to search through chat rooms to find out who was interested in that kind of thing when class ended and I had to log off.

I walked out with everyone else and watched as most of them got into their cars. Tony and Brian drove off separately. I waited in my car until Jennifer Pearson came out about fifteen minutes later and got into a silver Toyota Camry. I followed her out of the visitor parking lot and into the street, where I spotted Tony's van. I couldn't see through the tinted windows, but I knew Brian was in there, too. I pulled over and pretended to look through my purse as they passed me, but I needn't have bothered—I was invisible to them.

I pulled back into traffic and followed them at a distance. It wasn't hard to keep them in sight. Traffic was heavy and no one was driving fast. Jennifer drove to an apartment complex a few blocks away on Del Mar and into a security-gated underground garage. Tony parked across the street and I was forced to drive by.

I cruised around the block and parked several hundred feet behind his van. There were a few cars on the street between us, but I had an unobstructed view of both the van and the parking garage.

I had all my usual comfort items in the car with me—I'm used to commuting a fairly long distance, so I always carry a couple of bottles of water, a few snacks and my cell phone. I settled in and watched for about an hour. I could just imagine how antsy Brian must be. The passenger door of the van opened several times and was slammed shut, and once I thought I heard his whiney voice.

I wondered idly if Tony ever used the van for his exploits—if so, there would be evidence in it. Fibers, blood, secretions, they could all be identified and traced and help to put Tony away. I didn't know if he left any DNA traces on his victims—I watched TV and knew some rapists use protection just to guard against getting convicted. I toyed with the idea of an anonymous tip, but I knew that without probable cause, the cops couldn't search the van. And even the slightest tip-off and Tony could make the van and its contents disappear.

Then Tony did something risky—he got out of the van and walked up to the front of the building. I saw him checking the directory to find out which apartment was Jennifer's. I hoped she hadn't done anything stupid, like put her name out on the board. But even if all she did was list her initial, Tony would still be able to guess which one was hers. I didn't know how far he'd go, how brave his successes had made him.

I let out a breath when he came back and got into the van.

We sat there for another two hours. I could imagine Brian's impatience just as I could imagine the infinite depths of patience Tony would need. Tony would wait all night if he had to, taking note of everything that might aid or hinder his objective.

Finally Tony's van started up and left. There was no sign of Jennifer Pearson, and I surmised that she had simply spent the evening in. And maybe Brian had become so impatient that Tony couldn't wait around anymore either. I was about to call it a day myself, but I got an idea. I followed Tony's van at a discreet distance. For every move Tony made, I would be on his tail. Even if I couldn't get enough evidence on him to go to the cops, at least I would know what he was doing and where he was going. I wanted to be ready when the time came.

The time came sooner than I thought, a whole night sooner than Tony's original plan. Jennifer Pearson announced that Tuesday would be her final day of instruction and we would have another instructor, a guy from Oracle, for the last day. I saw Brian shoot Tony a confused look, and I couldn't wait to eavesdrop at lunch.

"So what are we gonna do now?" Brian asked over cheeseburgers and fries. I sat near them at the student food court again, behind the trusty palm leaves with a romance paperback on my table to deter approaches. Not that I needed to worry—a middle-aged woman alone might just as well be a fake ficus in a plastic pot, and I was well hidden, too. I could just see them through the leaves at an angle, but I didn't dare look over too often.

"I like to have enough time to do everything right, you know?" Tony said, keeping his voice down. I realized the planning was just as thrilling to him as the actual execution. I shuddered. If everything went according to his preliminary plans, tonight really would be an execution.

But maybe I had it all wrong. Maybe it was just some gruesome and ugly video game they were talking about. Maybe I was letting my imagination run away, wishing for something exciting in my life, something challenging.

"So I guess it's off, huh?" Brian sounded disappointed

at the prospect of not being able to participate in the rape, mutilation and murder of a woman. I knew then that it was real, that I had imagined none of it, that this time I had to do something.

Tony laughed, a low chuckle. "It's not off, man, we just have to tweak the plan a little. We can't count on her going out to celebrate with the class or anything. We gotta figure out some other way to get her to take the uh, you know."

"So, like, if we waste her anyway, why be so careful about it? Why not just do it without?" Brian's excited voice was high and Tony frowned, darting a nervous glance around to see if anyone had heard.

"No! Listen, fuckhead," he hissed. "We do it right or we don't do it at all. I need the pictures." Tony stopped talking.

"What?" Brian asked between bites. "What are you lookin' at?"

"Nothing, let's get outta here. I got a lot of stuff to think about." Tony threw the remains of his lunch into the trash and stalked off, Brian scrambling after him.

I figured Tony might like the admiration of a guy like Brian, but he was never going to risk getting caught over him. Brian was the expendable type.

Tony spent the afternoon listening attentively to Jennifer Pearson and taking notes. I couldn't see if they were work-related or had something to do with the big evening ahead of him, but I had a feeling he was busy planning. Brian just looked bored, leaning back in his chair, arms folded over him, staring out the window. I didn't want to know what was going through his small but vicious mind.

Jennifer Pearson's voice was strong and clear, and I

didn't need any help imagining a scream from her. But I knew she'd never get the chance to scream if Tony got that drug into her.

I was glad I kept my car stocked with necessities. Tony wasn't going to get this one—or anyone ever again—if I had my way.

When the class broke up at about three-thirty, I hung around and asked Jennifer if she had any big plans for the evening. She smiled indulgently, shook her head and said she would probably just stay in and order pizza or something. She checked her watch and gave me an impatient look. It was my last chance to warn her, but the words wouldn't come.

"Well, thanks for the class, then," I said lamely. "It's been real nice."

I walked out to my car and sat in it until I saw Tony's van pull out of the parking lot. Brian's car was right behind it. I followed them both a couple of blocks to the public parking off Lake Avenue. Brian left his car there and hopped into Tony's van. I gave them a head start before following discreetly in the direction of Jennifer's apartment. Tony parked half a block from the garage entrance and I slipped in five or six cars behind him.

I waited. While I waited I unwrapped my dinner, put on some soft music and popped a can of Diet Coke from my little ice chest. I had a nice, unobstructed view of the entrance to the apartment complex, and a pretty good view of the parking garage, too. If Jennifer did come out, either on foot or in her car, I would see her.

I was watching intently, so intently that I didn't notice what was right in front of my face. People did come and go, both on foot and in cars, and none of them were

Jennifer. But when Tony's van pulled out of its parking space and trundled down the street I nearly missed it. I spent a couple of seconds deciding what to do—should I follow Tony or stay and guard Jennifer? I watched as a pizza delivery boy walked up the front walk.

But there was something about the way the pizza guy walked, something cocky about his wiry frame. He was already up to the security gate when I recognized him. He was carrying a flat pizza box and a take-out bag. He set them on the block wall, fiddled with the gate and opened it. Brian followed a few seconds later.

I grabbed my bag, shoved my sunglasses on my face and put on my gloves. I had on a shapeless grey sweater and my bag was heavy, a scuffed canvas tote that had seen better days. I walked with a stooped, tired step to the front security gate and examined it. The lock was held open with a small piece of duct tape.

Jennifer's apartment was listed on the directory next to her name and I groaned. It was my good luck because I would know where to go, but it was a stupid, dangerous thing to do. If she lived, maybe I would tell her about it.

Tony must have already gone into the apartment and Brian was holding up the wall in the corridor. I waited at the directory, pretending to look for a particular address until Brian went into the apartment too.

Then I moved into high gear. Tony may have already subdued Jennifer in some way, whether by force or drugs. There wouldn't be much time. I pushed the door open a bit and peeked in. Brian had not locked the door, and I was grateful for his stupidity. Jennifer's apartment was clean and sparse, except for the empty pizza box spilled open across the beige carpet. There was no one in the living room

I pulled the gun out of my canvas tote and made sure the safety was off. It was a nice little pistol, a Beretta .380, just right for my small hands. I'd had it since I was young and pretty and learned the hard way that I had to protect myself from guys like Tony and Brian. Some rape victims go into therapy. Others go into a gun shop.

Tony and Brian were in the bedroom with Jennifer. She was limp and out cold, but I could see her labored breathing, so I knew she was still alive. They were taping her wrists to the bedposts with duct tape, their hands encased like mine in surgical gloves. Jennifer's tee shirt was torn and her jeans were yanked down. An open plastic bag was on the floor, what I had earlier mistaken for a take-out bag. I could see a variety of knives and a syringe sticking out of the bag. Like me, Tony must keep his stuff in his van. Risky, but then I know about risk.

"Get her panties off," Tony ordered, as he adjusted the camera. Brian grinned and pulled them down, then pulled on the cuffs of her jeans, disentangling her feet. He got the jeans off, then skimmed the panties off and tossed them on the floor. He yanked up her tee shirt and bra and fondled her breasts.

"Cut it out, Brian," Tony barked. "If you wanna help, you gotta do everything exactly right. Help me get her in position." Tony was sweating, his eyes bright and his voice hoarse. They pulled her legs apart and bent them at the knee. Tony adjusted her head so her face could be seen. There was a nasty bruise swelling up over one eye.

Brian ran his hands over her thighs. "C'mon, man, let's do her now." He started to unzip his jeans, his hard-on getting in the way.

"I said cut it out, fuckhead, unless you wanna get

hurt with the bitch!" Tony's script did not allow for Brian's ad libs.

It was time for me to do something. I pointed the gun at Tony and stepped into the room. "Put the camera down, Tony, unless you want to take my picture." I smiled sweetly.

Tony wheeled around to face me. He bared his teeth at me like an animal. "Get her," he ordered Brian.

But Brian knew a gun when he saw one and didn't move. "Aw, shit!" was all he said, his hard-on rapidly deflating.

"Get on the floor, Brian," I said to him. "Lie face down over there by the window and you won't get hurt." I turned the gun on him.

"Hey," he started babbling, "it wasn't my idea, it's Tony, he's the one with the website and everything. I never done nothing before, you gotta believe me, it's all Tony's idea, he's done it before, he's the one."

"Lie down, Brian, or I'll blow your head off." I savored the moment as Brian got down on the carpet, crying and whining.

"What'd you use on her, Tony?" I asked conversationally. "I don't think you had time to give her Rohypnol in a drink. Did you inject her with something?" I aimed the gun at his belly button.

"What do you want?" Tony asked. He still had the little digital camera in his hands and I could see the wheels turning in his sick brain.

"Drop the camera and we'll talk." I didn't want my picture to appear anywhere but I didn't want to shoot him, either.

He set the camera down on the bed and smiled at me. "There. Satisfied?"

"No, not really," I replied. "I think we both know what you have to do next. Go ahead and get the syringe. If you touch one of those knifes, though, even a little bit, I'll blow a hole in your belly and watch you die. It takes a gut-shot person a long time to bleed to death, and I'd get to watch every minute of it. Of course, most folks go into shock right away and spoil the fun, so I might even take your picture to remember it, if I can figure out your little camera."

He looked puzzled.

I sighed. I hate dealing with these stupid kids sometimes. "Get the syringe, Tony. Shoot Brian with the drug if there's any left. Make him be quiet!" That incessant whining was getting on my nerves.

He hesitated.

I moved in a little closer and pointed the gun in his face. "Do it now, asshole."

He bent down and pulled the syringe out of the bag. It was a small one, the kind diabetics use to shoot their insulin doses.

"There isn't any more," he lied. "I only brought enough for this one, uh, time."

"Do you know what an embolism is, Tony? If there isn't any more drug, you're gonna have to shoot Brian with air. You know what that'll do, don't you?"

"Jesus, you're crazy," Tony whispered. I smiled.

Brian's whimpers grew louder, more articulate. "Get the other drug, Tony," he cried. "I know you have some. Use it all, I don't wanna die. Just put me out like you did the bitch. Please, Tony!"

Tony shrugged. "Whatever, man." He reached down slowly into the bag and drew out a vial. "This is the heavy duty stuff, dude," he said. "It might be more than you can do."

"Please, Tony," Brian begged again. "I don't care, just put me out!"

"That's it, Tony," I crooned. "Nice and easy, no sharp movements, no reason for me to blow that goddamn smirk off your ugly face."

Tony filled the syringe and held it out so I could see it.

"Okay, Tony-boy, go shoot your partner. Then lay the syringe right by him. Do everything slowly so I can see it. If you move too fast, I'll kill you both and call the cops. They'll probably give me a medal or something."

Tony did as he was told and Brian's whimpers ceased. "Now what?" he said.

I grinned. "Now the really fun part. Step back." He stumbled back a couple of steps. Keeping the gun trained on him, I pulled the plastic bag toward me. I found the largest knife in the bag and pulled it out.

"Turn around," I ordered. He hesitated again.

"Just turn around and pick up the camera. We're going to take some pictures."

He turned around and bent over to get the camera from the bed. I dropped the gun in my sweater pocket. Then using both hands I shoved the knife into the middle of his back with such force I could feel it slide on a bone. He made a raspy noise and his arms flew back to grab at the knife, then he fell forward onto the bed and twitched. I reached under him and pulled the camera out. It took a few minutes for him to stop moving. Long minutes. It always seems like an eternity when you're waiting for that last twitch.

It was very quiet. Jennifer's breathing was the only

sound I could hear.

I took a deep breath myself and put the gun back into my bag. Then I examined the camera. It was digital, fairly straightforward and I checked the memory. Several pictures had already been taken, pictures of Brian. I set it and took several close-ups of Jennifer, being careful to avoid getting any part of Tony in the shots. Then I wiped the camera, pulled the tape off Jennifer's wrists and put her fingerprints on the knife in Tony's back. It was slow going. She was dead weight, figuratively speaking. After I had obtained a good impression of her grip on the knife in Tony's back, I let her fall to the floor and got Tony's prints on the camera.

I checked my watch. I had been in Jennifer Pearson's apartment for less than fifteen minutes. Jennifer was alive, Tony was dead and Brian was out with a shot of drugs. Good work for one evening.

I left quietly by the front door, leaving it open an inch or so. As I went out the gate I was gratified to see the little piece of duct tape still holding the lock open. The cops wouldn't miss it, either.

I got into my car, peeled off my gloves and drove past Tony's van. Resisting the urge to look in it, I drove to Lake Avenue. I put my canvas bag in the trunk and did some shopping. I felt so much better.

As I walked past the store windows, I thought about what would happen. Jennifer would wake up and start screaming, then call the police. She wouldn't remember much of anything, but the evidence would tell the story. Two men had posed as pizza delivery persons and attacked her in her apartment. They had drugged her, but medical examination would confirm that she had not been raped.

She had managed to free herself and stab one of her attackers. The other one was drugged to the gills with God-knows-what and if he survived the overdose wouldn't exactly be a credible witness. The syringe and bag of knives would be discovered, as would the camera with the pictures. Brian would talk about the website and Tony's van would be searched. The stupid fuckhead would get what he deserved.

I smiled at my faint reflection in the shop windows. There are so many smart people, but even at Caltech, it doesn't always take a genius to make things right.

Neither beginner's luck nor an old tout's wisdom could predict the outcome of our next story, where a day at the races becomes a day to die. The racetrack in question is **Santa Anita Park,** *a turquoise and cream colored, art deco gem nestled at the base of the San Gabriel foothills. This elegant landmark to the sport of kings was designed in the thirties by Gordon Kaufmann, famed architect of the Times-Mirror building, and Hoover Dam. The beautifully landscaped grounds are highlighted by the fragrant Paddock Gardens, where a bronze statue of Seabiscuit, the big-hearted little champion stands proudly. Everywhere you walk, you hear the hum, and feel the pulse—"Go, baby, go!" Inside the Club House, gamblers and first-timers line up to place their bets as the aroma of carved roast beef sandwiches mingles with cigarette smoke and draft beer. Follow the glamorous elite to the exclusive Turf Club where the celebrity ghosts of Clark and Bing, Cary and Fred haunt their old stomping grounds. There's no place in L.A. quite like Santa Anita Park. To quote a popular phrase—"Whatever the occasion, Santa Anita delivers." In our case, it's murder...*

"THE BEST LAID SCHEMES . . . "
by Jinx Beers

Some seedy looking joe about five foot six shoves a twenty and a single into my cage and croaks: "Five on five, six on six, ten on ten."

It takes me only a moment to figure out what he wants and hit the keys on the pari-mutuel machine to spit out a five-dollar ticket on entry number five, three two-dollar bets for entry number six, and ten dollars on horse number ten. I slide the five tickets toward him with one hand and pull his money back toward me with the other, slipping it quickly into the cash drawer. The transaction concludes in less than thirty seconds and I'm ready for the next sucker standing in front of my betting window at Santa Anita Race Track during the Oak Tree Meet.

My wife also works the Santa Anita meet in the clubhouse, serving cocktails to people who think, because they own a race horse, they have a right to whatever else they want. Most of them have so much money they don't know what to do with it, so they buy each other drinks and meals until the races have been run and their fortunes for that day have been increased or decreased accordingly. OK, not every horse owner is rich. But the ones who aren't don't go to the clubhouse either.

On her breaks my wife sometimes slips out to a betting window to place a small wager on a sure thing. Nothing's really a sure thing, but an even money bet or less is as safe as they come. She wins most of the time, tiny sums, but just the act of winning can be very satisfying if you're not a big gambler.

My best friend works the gift shop at Santa Anita, across from my betting window, which is not inside as most are, but at the end of the saddling paddock outside. It's unobtrusive, but available for those who want to place a bet and either can't tear themselves away from the glorious grounds, or want to watch the horses being saddled for the next race.

Santa Anita Park is not only gorgeous to look at but steeped in tradition, from the beautiful fountain that greets you as you enter through the turnstile, to the statue of the immortal Seabiscuit standing watch in the middle of the walking ring. The hedges are so mature they create a maze-like atmosphere, and from a distance even the topiary horse and jockey look as if they could fly down the track with the best of the Thoroughbreds.

Two weeks ago I happen to glance over the shoulder of the person in line and see my wife sidle up to my best friend in front of the gift shop and whisper in his ear. He nods and they turn away from each other to carry on their own jobs. I do a double take, wondering what they're cooking up. I've never seen them whispering to each other before, and they both know I don't like surprises.

* * *

My friend and I meet when we're ten years old and end up going to the same college. When we graduate we look for jobs together. No way could we guess within a few weeks both of us would find employment at a racetrack.

We visit the opening day of the regular season, right after Christmas, and spot a sign in the gift shop indicating they're looking for help. Upon inquiry, it happens the assistant manager has been in a car accident the day before and the owner is trying to handle everything himself with one clerk. My friend has a major in finance and although he never would have considered being a clerk in a store, stepping into an assistant manager job at a famous race track appeals to him. He isn't a hard worker, which he readily admits, and figures this could be a cushy job with a livable income and possibly some way to bolster that in the future. With his degree in finance and his willingness to work for a minimum stipend, he's hired on the spot and starts work that day. I envy him his job, as I still don't have one, and find myself at the track more often than not.

Having very little money I'm not betting much, but occasionally blow a couple of bucks on a long shot hoping to score some pocket money. In between races I hang around the gift shop and when my friend isn't busy with customers or the books, we shoot the gab.

A couple of weeks into the meet, my friend tells me the track has a program for apprentice pari-mutuel clerks, and I should go to the office and check it out. He hands me a slip of paper folded in half and directs me toward the management section of the track.

In a nutshell, the note is an introduction, I'm eventually hired into the program, go to pari-mutuel school, and become the guy you think is going to sell you the ticket on the winning horse that's going to make you rich. You know the joke at the race track? "How do you become a millionaire? Start with two million and work down!"

* * *

That is nearly ten years ago. Now I can count money, punch keys, make change, and cash in winners in my sleep. And my friend is manager of the gift shop and appears to be doing very well indeed.

I meet my wife at the track, of course. She hires on in the clubhouse about three years into my own employment. My friend and I both find her enjoyable to look at and court her, but in the end I'm the one she picks to marry. Still, we practically become a trio: me, my wife and my best friend.

Everything seems fine until a couple of weeks ago when I begin to suspect something is going on between them. More than once I see them whispering to each other, but when I ask what is going on, neither of them admit to any thing "going on" at all.

A week ago last Wednesday evening when I arrive home, I walk into the den while my wife is talking on the telephone. She jumps, as if she's startled, and quickly says, "Gotta go now," and hangs up. When I ask who she's been talking to, she shrugs and says, "No one you know."

Three days later after I finish up at work, I walk out to my car in the parking lot and catch my best friend leaning against the door talking to my wife through the window. She is already seated and waiting for me. When he sees me, he waves goodbye and quickly walks away without saying a word.

Sunday I see them with their heads together at Sirona's, the restaurant under the stands across the way, when I go over on my break for a sandwich. They're smiling into each other's eyes and nodding.

OK, I think, my wife and my best friend are having an affair. Here I am approaching middle age, a birthday coming up soon, and I'm losing my wife to my best friend. Do they really believe I'm so stupid I wouldn't notice? If I'd caught them several times together, how many times have there been that I don't know about?

It's possible. We don't have exactly the same time off. Sometimes my wife drives her own car, telling me she's going to visit her sister after work. And she has an additional day off. I work five days a week, she only has to be at the track four. Although we're both off on Mondays and Tuesdays when the track is dark, she doesn't work Wednesdays either.

Some Wednesdays my best friend isn't in the gift shop all day, and when I ask, he says he was off buying or picking up new merchandise. Always Wednesday. Of course Wednesday is the lightest attendance day, building up through the week toward heavy duty weekends, so it would be the logical day for him to tend to business.

* * *

Yesterday, a Wednesday, I come home from work, see my front door ajar and my wife dead on the kitchen floor. Her throat has been cut, apparently with one of our own carving knives. Blood is everywhere. The house has been ransacked.

At first glance the police say it looks like an invasion robbery that has gone very wrong. Possibly, the police say, my wife returned to the house in the midst of the robbery and paid the ultimate price. I break down, crying. After all, no matter if she is having a dalliance elsewhere, I love my wife. The tears are real; I have lost the love of my life.

The police check for fingerprints in the house and find mine, my wife's, my best friend's, the housekeeper's who comes every Friday morning, and some strange prints around the sink. Those last prints turn out to belong to a plumber who the housekeeper calls to open up a stopped-up drain. The plumber is the housekeeper's cousin and she gets the work done free.

Maybe, the police speculate, the robbers wear gloves.

The police also check alibis. Mine, my best friend's, the house cleaner's and the plumber's.

Although the police can't pin down the exact time of death, the autopsy determines it occurred two to three hours after breakfast, based on the contents of her stomach. I tell them she hasn't eaten breakfast yet when I leave the house for work that morning, about nine o'clock. Our daily routine when we drive together is to leave early enough to stop for breakfast somewhere and be at the track with plenty of time for me to check out my till without having to rush. For her to have eaten breakfast after nine was the regular time she had breakfast. It made sense.

What the police don't know is that my wife has actually eaten breakfast about seven at home with me. I persuaded her I didn't feel too good and didn't want to have anything greasy for breakfast. I have only some toast and coffee and leave the house about nine, my usual time.

No one notices a bundle weighted with silverware, jewelry, and a small coin collection I surreptitiously drop over the bridge into muddy Devil's Gate Dam, only a short detour before getting to work. Right on time.

* * *

Having been away a couple of days on a buying trip, today my best friend comes over to my betting window as I take a quick break. He's distressed and says he's just heard about the tragedy of my wife's death from a friend in the business office. I glare at him hoping he's suffering as much as I am, at least until I can take care of him, too.

"My god," he says. "How could you be at work today? I can't believe this has happened! We had everything planned. I'd gotten the plane tickets; she'd made the hotel reservations. She practically had the bags packed!"

My best friend covers his face with his hands to hide his tears. I can't understand his boldness, to grieve right in front of me. Anger wells up and I clench my fists at my side. It's all I can do to stop myself from striking out at him right then and there.

Looking over his shoulder I see two burly uniformed Arcadia policemen and the plainclothes detective handling the case approaching. As I listen to the words of my best friend, my face crumbles, tears spring to my eyes, my heart beats faster, and I begin to sweat. *What have I done?* I think.

"It was perfect," he says. "She said as your best friend, I knew you better than anyone else besides her and could help make the plans without you ever catching on. We knew you had a suspicious mind, but we were so casual

around you, and you never seemed to react. She was sure
you didn't have any idea what we were planning together.
We were so careful.

"The two of you in Hawaii together for two whole
weeks. It would have been a perfect surprise birthday
present for you. We've been best friends most of our lives,
and your wife loved you dearly. We wanted to do something
really special for you this year. And now this has happened!"

*The University of Southern California, locally known as **USC**, is world-renowned for its research facilities and Hollywood celebrity alumni, but the University's athletic program often grabs more of the media spotlight. The long-standing rivalry between USC and UCLA is legendary, and the Trojan marching band even played with the rock band Fleetwood Mac.*

For over one hundred years, Trojan football has played a major role at the sprawling University Park campus located adjacent to Exposition Park in downtown L.A. The mascot colors are the famous crimson and gold, but on one fatal evening at the landmark campus, the USC colors took on a new meaning when blood spilled crimson in the golden glint of greed...

SETUP
by Pamela Samuels-Young

Larry Littlefield gazed at the husky white man sitting across from him, confident that if he studied the stern, hawkish face long enough, he could detect some sign that the man was trying to play him. Littlefield considered himself a pretty decent attorney, but not even he believed he was good enough to have a high-profile case like this dropped in his lap.

"So, tell me," Littlefield said, tugging at his goatee, "out of all the attorneys in L.A., why do you want me to represent you?"

Officer Harold McIntyre, a barrel-shaped man with pockmarked cheeks, sat up straighter in his chair, as if to brace himself for a grilling. "You represented an officer out of Southwest in a race discrimination case a while back," he said. His voice had a raspy hum, like he had a handful of gravel rolling around inside his mouth. "And I've seen you on the news quite a bit."

Littlefield liked having his skills acknowledged. He operated under the principle that if you can't beat 'em in court, then bash 'em in the press.

"Your case could end up being bigger than Rodney King," Littlefield replied. "For the record, murder trials aren't exactly my specialty." He neglected to mention that he didn't have a specialty.

The first flicker of emotion surfaced on the man's face, but Littlefield didn't know whether it was the Rodney King comparison or the mention of the word "murder" that made him flinch.

"I don't need an attorney with experience trying murder cases," McIntyre said calmly. "This case isn't going to trial. If it does, I'm a dead man."

Littlefield almost wanted to laugh. The case *was* going to trial and McIntyre *was* a dead man. The shooting of Deon Jackson, the University of Southern California's star running back and recent Heisman Trophy winner, had left virtually the entire city in a state of mourning. Even white folks were calling his death a textbook example of what was wrong with the LAPD. Luckily for McIntyre, nobody had caught it on videotape.

"Tell me why you think it's not going to trial. You hoping to cut a deal?"

McIntyre shook his head so hard Littlefield thought he felt the room vibrate. "The shooting was clean. The only hope I have of proving that is by getting my side of the story to the public. You have a reputation for being good at that."

Littlefield knew McIntyre had another reason for wanting to hire him. Black folks, especially those in South Central, didn't trust cops. Having a black man as his mouthpiece would add credibility to his story. Since McIntyre didn't have his own race card to play, he wanted to borrow Littlefield's.

"According to the papers," Littlefield challenged, "Jackson was unarmed. How's that a clean shooting?"

McIntyre hesitated. "Is our conversation confidential? Are you saying you'll represent me?"

"I can't decide that until I hear what you have to say." Littlefield enjoyed hearing the neediness in McIntyre's voice. He had never felt that kind of power over a cop before. "But whatever you tell me is still protected by the attorney-client privilege."

Officer McIntyre inhaled and looked down at his hands. "I was on solo patrol, driving around the perimeter of the University, when I saw two black guys . . . uh . . . I mean, two young guys, standing near a tree in Exposition Park. I figured they were making a drug deal."

"You always assume a drug deal is going down when you see two brothers standing near a tree?"

Officer McIntyre's beefy neck turned a deep crimson. "I could tell from the way they kept looking around that they were up to something. So, I pulled over and jumped out. One guy took off deeper into the park, the other one ran across Exposition Boulevard, back toward the campus. So I took off after him."

"Did you know then that it was Jackson you were chasing?"

Officer McIntyre responded with a solemn shake of his head. After a long moment, Littlefield made a circular motion with his index finger, directing him to continue.

"Like I said, I ran after him, yelling 'LAPD.' I was gaining on him and—"

"Hold up." Littlefield raised his right hand. "You expect me to believe that the best college running back in the nation couldn't outrun you?"

"Maybe he was high, or maybe he wasn't giving it his all, I don't know," McIntyre said, his jaw line tightening. "I'm just telling you what happened. When Jackson got to the edge of the campus, he stopped near some bushes, turned back and aimed a gun at me. That's when I fired."

"But there was no gun found at the scene," Littlefield pointed out.

"I don't know what happened to it, but I'm telling you I saw one." McIntyre paused. "You ever have a gun pointed at you? That's not something you can forget."

Littlefield certainly agreed with that. Recalling his own run-in with a cop and a gun made him distrust McIntyre even more. "So what do you think happened to the gun?"

McIntyre lowered his voice an octave. "You want to know what I think?" he said, leaning forward, as if poised to reveal some sinister plot. "I think somebody from the University got to the scene and took it. And they're willing to hang me out to dry to cover up the fact that their little Heisman Trophy winner was out buying drugs and carrying a concealed weapon."

"Didn't you go look for the gun yourself?"

"I'd never shot anybody before. I was in a state of shock. Before I knew it, the campus police were everywhere. They went nuts when they saw it was Jackson. I told 'em he had a gun. I just assumed it had flown out of his hand and was somewhere in the vicinity, probably in the bushes. And I bet the campus police found it." McIntyre's eyes narrowed. "But instead of turning it over, they kept it."

Littlefield wasn't buying a word of McIntyre's story. "According to the news reports I heard, it was too dark for you to have seen a gun in Jackson's hands."

"There was more than enough light from the streetlamps," McIntyre insisted, his voice louder than it should have been. He sighed, then sat back in his chair. "So will you take my case?"

"If all you want is a chance to get your story to the public, why aren't you talking to somebody like Gloria Allred or Leo Terrell?"

"I don't think Allred likes men and I know Terrell hates cops."

"What about Mark Geragos or Tom Mesereau?"

"Can't afford 'em."

Indecision gripped Littlefield. The media attention he'd get from handling the case would be major. But he would be vilified by the black community for defending the man—the white man—who murdered one of their own. Black folks were his bread and butter. If they stopped knocking on his door, he'd starve to death. As much as the case intrigued him, the risks outweighed the rewards.

Before he could communicate his decision to McIntyre, the officer pulled an envelope from his back pocket and slid it across the desk. "Here's a cashier's check for my retainer," he said. "But I have to be straight with you, this is all the money I can get my hands on at the moment."

Littlefield opened the envelope and stared at a check in the amount of twenty thousand dollars made out to him. The clients he represented didn't have account balances with that many zeroes. Every case he took was on contingency. An instant twenty grand in his pocket would solve a whole lot of problems.

He promptly calculated that, at his rate of $250 an hour, the retainer would cover exactly eighty hours of billable time. If he worked the case hard, the retainer would be spent in three, four weeks tops. He could do a little investigating, hold a few press conferences, then tell McIntyre to find himself a new lawyer.

Littlefield laid the check down on his desk and looked up. "Officer McIntyre," he said, extending his hand, "you've got yourself a lawyer."

Just before dusk, three hours after McIntyre walked out of his office, Littlefield eased his Mercedes Benz into a metered parking space on the east side of the USC campus. He grabbed a small note pad from his glove box and climbed out of the car.

Littlefield hit the alarm button on his key ring, took a few steps, then looked back and hit it again. He had to be doubly sure that the most expensive item he owned, to the extent you owned a leased vehicle, was secure.

As he entered the University's Figueroa Street gate, he felt a twinge of *déjà vu*. He'd grown up near 36th and Normandie in the low-income neighborhood that surrounded the campus. Then and now, entering the grounds of the private university was like stepping into another world, one with stately brick buildings, colorful flowers, and smiling white girls with long flowing hair right out of some shampoo commercial.

He headed up Child's Way, passing Doheny Library on the right and the Administration building on the left. He stopped just a few feet from Tommy Trojan, the school mascot. Back in the day, when the campus was practically deserted on Sunday afternoons, he would climb upon the bronze statue and pretend that he was a star Trojan, catching the game-winning pass. His fantasy. Deon Jackson's reality.

He made a left on Trousdale Parkway, and as he neared the edge of the campus, the side that bordered Exposition Park, he spotted a makeshift memorial to the dead football player. From where he stood, he could see a bunch of wilted flowers and a poster-size picture of Jackson resting against a short brick post. An uneasy feeling deep in his gut kept him from going any closer.

Littlefield looked out across Exposition Boulevard, hoping to spot the tree where Deon and the presumed drug dealer had supposedly met, but there were trees everywhere. He turned back toward the campus and tried to guess where McIntyre had been standing when he fired at Jackson. The entire scene suddenly depressed him and he wanted nothing to do with the case.

But he had already deposited McIntyre's check, and he needed the money. So he would do what he had to do.

Two days later, at ten in the morning, Littlefield and Officer McIntyre gathered before a horde of reporters on the steps of the African-American Museum, just across the street from the USC campus. The idea to hold the press conference at the museum had come to him during his visit to the USC campus. He had sent out press releases the next day and spent hours writing and rewriting his statement.

As Littlefield watched the gathering news media, he was flush with excitement. His press conferences had never attracted a crowd like this. He spotted news vans from the three major networks, as well as several local TV and radio reporters, including one from NPR. Littlefield grinned. He should be paying McIntyre for this opportunity.

Gus Washington, a reporter for the *Los Angeles Sentinel*, the city's African-American newspaper, gave him a barely discernible nod. Littlefield nodded back. Despite the physical distance between them, Littlefield could see the disapproval in Washington's eyes.

When Littlefield finally stepped up to the semi-circle of microphones, the buzz of the crowd immediately subsided. "We called this press conference today," he began, nervously shuffling the three index cards in his hands, "to tell Officer McIntyre's story. But before I do that, I'd like to tell you why we're gathered here on the steps of the African-American Museum."

He paused to clear his throat as the note he'd written down on the first index card instructed him to do. "This museum is symbolic of the struggles of the African-American residents of South Central. A struggle Officer McIntyre has personally witnessed during the eighteen years he has served this community."

Littlefield noticed that the reporters were already getting antsy. He didn't want them pelting him with questions before he finished his prepared remarks, so he picked up his pace.

"Nothing in Officer McIntyre's record would suggest that he has ever done anything other than what he was paid to do—protect and serve this primarily African-American community. As we all know, the most fundamental principle of our judicial system is innocent until proven guilty . . . something many of you in the media seem to have forgotten. My client—"

"Deon Jackson was unarmed," someone yelled from the back of the crowd. "How do you explain that?"

Littlefield held up both hands. "If you could just wait until—"

"And that cop's record ain't exactly squeaky clean!" Roy Smith, a member of the civil rights organization, No Justice, No Peace, stepped forward, waving a piece of paper in his hand. "This ain't the first time your client was accused of misconduct. What about the beating of Preston Scott? Looks like your client's graduated from beating young black men to shooting 'em!"

Preston Scott? Littlefield shot a glance in McIntyre's direction. The man's neck had turned bright red again.

Roy Smith was a semi-senile rabble-rouser, but he usually had his facts straight. The reporters were all looking at Smith now, more interested in what he had to say.

"Uh–I–I'd like to finish my prepared statement before answering any questions." Littlefield glanced down at his notes and tried to remember where he had left off. "Deon Jackson isn't the only victim here," he said, his voice shaky now. "When all the facts are known—"

"You don't usually defend police abuse cases," another reporter called out. "Why did you decide to take this one?"

"Because, just like you, I'm interested in making sure justice is done."

Littlefield fought off the urge to smile. That short sound bite would probably lead off one of the local newscasts later that evening. As more questions came his way, many more than he wanted to answer, he decided to use the only power he had. The power to leave them hungry for more. "That's it for now," he said, stuffing the index cards in his breast pocket and motioning for McIntyre to follow him.

They darted off as the reporters began shouting questions simultaneously, the rush of their voices folding into a chorus of gibberish.

* * *

As he shaved and dressed the next morning, Littlefield mulled over what McIntyre had told him about Preston Scott. Six months earlier, the teenager had accused the officer of throwing him to the ground after a routine traffic stop and repeatedly kicking him in the ribs. An Internal Affairs investigation, however, had failed to substantiate Scott's allegations.

Littlefield didn't sweat it. He would simply play the hand he'd been dealt. He headed for the tiny kitchen of his two-bedroom apartment and poured himself a cup of coffee. His current live-in girlfriend, Desiree, always made him coffee before leaving for her job as a teller at Citibank. He took a sip, then walked to the front door to retrieve the *Times*, anxious to see if he'd made the front page. He had missed the evening news and fallen asleep before the start of the eleven o'clock broadcasts.

When he opened the door and looked down for the newspaper, he realized that someone had stolen it again. Littlefield cursed and slammed the door. As soon as he made some real money, he was moving out of Inglewood and into a house where somebody would have to climb ten-foot gates and get past two Rottweilers to steal his newspaper.

Littlefield didn't leave for his storefront office on Manchester Boulevard until almost eleven. On the way, he stopped at a strip mall to pick up a *Times* and was thrilled to find his face on page one, just below the fold. He bought six copies, along with a tuna sandwich and a root beer. After wolfing down his lunch, he made some quick notes for his two o'clock meeting at the D.A.'s office.

* * *

When Deputy District Attorney Shana Banks walked into the lobby, she looked nothing like Littlefield had expected. She had dark, wavy, shoulder-length hair and an Asian-Hawaiian look about her. Littlefield thought he saw a hint of Africa mixed up in there too, but he wasn't sure. Whatever she was, he liked it.

She led him into a drab little conference room and they sat facing each other at a table scarred with graffiti. "Here's a copy of the police report," she said. "The autopsy and the ballistics report aren't in yet, but you'll get them as soon as I do. I don't usually conduct my document exchanges in person, but I had to meet the brother who had the balls to defend Deon Jackson's killer."

Littlefield smiled. So she was black. "My client's guilt hasn't been proven in a court of law yet."

"It will be," she said with a smile. "Unless he decides to plead."

She had a slight cockiness about her, but Littlefield didn't find it offensive. A whiff of some overly feminine fragrance tickled his nose. Maybe the case would actually go to trial. He'd like to smell her all day long.

"Well," Littlefield said, "copping a plea isn't in the plan at the moment."

Shana smiled again. "I heard about your press conference yesterday. Your client shot an unarmed, superstar athlete who just happened to be out for a late night jog. You don't really want to try this case, do you?"

Hell yeah, if I get to see you every day. "I'll do whatever I have to do to prove that my client responded appropriately to a legitimate threat against his life." Littlefield could not take his eyes off the woman.

"May I ask you a question?" Shana said.

"Certainly."

"Why are you staring at me like that?"

"I'm sorry." Littlefield shifted in his seat, not at all embarrassed. "I'm sure you hear this all the time, but you're a very attractive woman. Mind if I ask your ethnicity?"

Shana rolled her eyes and pursed her lips. "I'd heard that you were quite the charmer. Do you use this stuff on your male opponents, too?"

Littlefield chucked. "No, really. I'm just curious."

"If you really want to know," she said, folding her arms across her chest, "my mother's Filipino and my father's black."

"Okay, okay," Littlefield said, nodding. "So you got that Tiger Woods thing going on."

Shana sighed. "So, is that it?"

"I guess it is." Littlefield stood up, but he did not want to leave. "I hope we have an opportunity to talk again real soon."

When Littlefield got back to his office, he had a voice mail message from Officer McIntyre. He started to feel guilty about taking the man's money, but the feeling passed in about five seconds. He dialed his client's number.

"I just got some very important information," McIntyre said in an urgent tone. "Do you mind meeting me at my house? I don't want to discuss this on the phone."

Littlefield wasn't thrilled about having to drive to Orange County in rush-hour traffic, but at least he could bill McIntyre for the drive time.

Ninety minutes later, when he pulled up in front of McIntyre's two-story, Craftsman-style home, Littlefield marveled at the size of the place. *How in the hell could he afford to live like this on a cop's salary?*

McIntyre's wife showed Littlefield past a living room filled with antiques and into a spacious den with a fully stocked bar and a fifty-inch plasma TV. When Littlefield finished examining the room, he wished he had asked for a larger retainer.

McIntyre trudged into the room wearing an agitated expression. "The autopsy report showed drugs in Jackson's system," he said, as they sat down on a worn leather sofa. "But the Coroner's Office destroyed it and replaced it with one that didn't."

"Where'd you hear that?" Littlefield asked.

"I'm a cop. I have friends."

Littlefield wondered whether McIntyre's information was credible. "Exactly who had it destroyed?"

"I don't know. But USC certainly has that kind of pull."

"What kind of drugs?"

"I don't know that either."

They talked for about thirty minutes, then Littlefield headed back to his car. He pulled into a nearby 7-Eleven to buy himself another root beer. As he waited in line to pay for it, his mind flooded with possibilities. What if the University *had* set up McIntyre to protect the image of their star running back? And what if Littlefield exposed the cover-up?

As he walked out of the store, he heard someone call out his name.

"Mr. Littlefield," chirped a thin white man, rushing up to him. "I just wanted to say thanks."

Littlefield looked over his shoulder to make sure the man was talking to him.

"I know it took some guts for you to come to the defense of that cop," the man said, extending his hand. "I don't particularly care for attorneys, but you're A-OK with me."

Littlefield hesitated, then reached out and shook the man's outstretched hand. Before he could get to his car, he noticed more people—white people—smiling at him. *This was certainly a switch.*

As he headed up Katella Boulevard and onto the 605 Freeway, the Jackson case was suddenly taking on a whole new meaning for him.

Littlefield got little sleep that night, obsessed with the direction his career would take if he could actually prove that the all-powerful University of Southern California was involved in a major cover-up. He got to his office before nine for the first time in weeks. As soon as he opened the door, he spotted a blank envelope just inside the doorway.

He picked it up. The single sheet of paper inside contained three typed words: *Check the glass.* Littlefield studied it for several seconds. Was the note referring to the Jackson case? He pulled out the police report and looked for a reference to glass. There was none. *Check the glass.* What glass?

It took him twenty-five minutes to get to the USC campus and another fifteen to find a parking space. He jogged over to the location where Deon Jackson was gunned down and saw that the wilted flowers had been replaced with fresh ones, mostly lilies, daffodils and carnations. He carefully scanned the area, hoping to spot some clue he had missed before. This time, he ventured closer to the spot where Jackson had fallen. When he heard a crunching sound underneath his feet, a chill ran through him. He looked down and saw small shards of broken glass. *Check the glass.*

He squatted down close to the ground and assumed he was looking at the remains of a broken bottle. But when he picked up one of the pieces, he saw imprints of lines. *Check the glass.* He looked around to see if he could determine where the glass might have come from. Nothing registered. But then he looked up and saw that the streetlight directly above him was busted.

With his pulse in overdrive, Littlefield pulled out his cell phone and called his client.

After a single knock on McIntyre's front door, the officer snatched it open. Littlefield excitedly showed him the glass he had collected in a discarded Starbucks cup.

"What's this?" McIntyre asked.

"Glass I found at the scene of the shooting."

"This is what you wanted to show me? So what does it mean?"

Littlefield had his theory all worked out, but wanted to see just how good a cop McIntyre was. He handed him the note. "You tell me."

He followed as McIntyre walked over to his living room couch, staring at the note. The officer looked up at Littlefield, puzzled. Littlefield was so keyed up he couldn't wait for McIntyre to connect the dots. "The streetlight," he said. "This glass is from the streetlight right above the area where the shooting happened. Look at the ridges."

McIntyre picked up a small piece. "I still don't understand what this means."

Littlefield pointed at the note. "Somebody slid that note underneath my door. Somebody's trying to help you."

"How?"

"You said the area was well lit, that you had a clear view of Jackson holding a gun. But everybody who's examined the scene claims it was too dark."

McIntyre shrugged, still confused.

"But it wasn't. Somebody busted out that streetlight." Littlefield paused for dramatic effect. "*After* the shooting."

The realization of what his attorney was telling him slowly spread across McIntyre's face.

"That streetlight would've lit up the area like a searchlight," Littlefield continued. "But somebody busted it out because they want people to think it was too dark for you to have seen a gun in Jackson's hand."

"I told you!" McIntyre's voice cracked. "Somebody's trying to frame me."

Littlefield reached out and squeezed McIntyre's shoulder. "But we're not going to let them get away with it."

Littlefield spent the rest of the day at his office, trying to come up with some clever gimmick for his next press conference. He headed home just after seven. As he climbed the steps to his apartment, he sensed a presence behind him. Before he could turn around, someone snatched his hands behind his back and tightly wound his wrists with what felt like wire.

"What the hell! Let go of me!" Littlefield struggled wildly and was about to yell out again, when a big hand clamped down over his mouth and a hood encased his head in darkness.

Littlefield felt himself being dragged backwards down the stairs, then tossed face down into the back seat of a car. "What the hell are you doing?" he shouted.

He heard both the driver-side door and the front passenger door open and close. "You'll be back home in a sec," said a gruff voice, as the car started moving.

When Littlefield tried to raise his head, he felt something hard slam into the base of his skull, causing him to yell out in pain.

"You need to stop nosing around," said a voice from the driver's seat. "Your client shot that kid and that's just the way it is. You better plead him out or you'll be sharing a box in the ground with Deon Jackson. You got it?"

Littlefield took a long time to speak. His nose was pressed into the seat and he could barely breathe through the hood. He wanted to turn sideways to get some air, but his head felt too heavy to lift. "So basically, you're admitting that my client was framed," he mumbled nervously, "but you want me to keep quiet about it."

"You apparently weren't listening," the driver groused. "I never said anything about anybody being framed."

Something crashed into the back of his head again. This time, he saw tiny gold stars.

Littlefield was so paralyzed by the pain that he seemed to lose track of time. In what seemed like only a minute or so later, the car stopped and Littlefield was hurled to the ground, head first.

* * *

Littlefield sat at the Formica table in his kitchen as Desiree used a Q-tip to dab Bactine on the ugly bruise just below his left eye.

"I think we should call the police," she said. The panic in her voice mirrored the terrified look on her face. "What if they come back?"

"They're not coming back. At least not tonight."

"You don't know that. What if—"

Littlefield raised his hand. "I ain't calling the police." He pressed an ice pack against the back of his head and tried to think. He did not want to abandon the case. He was apparently close to exposing what somebody desperately wanted to hide. He felt scared for McIntyre, and even more so for himself. But a defiant curiosity had taken hold of him, encouraging him to stay the course.

Desiree folded her arms and pouted. Littlefield reminded himself that he had to start dating smarter women. Right now, he needed a female who could help him with the pros and cons of his situation. Somebody like Shana Banks.

"I don't understand why you're even representing that man," Desiree said. "You know he killed that boy. Everybody I know is calling you an Uncle Tom."

Littlefield thought about explaining what the case would do for his career or telling Desiree about his suspicions of a cover-up, but his head hurt too much. "Could you get me a glass of wine?" he said instead.

Desiree did as requested, but her lips kept flapping. "How in the hell can that cop claim Deon Jackson had a gun? That boy didn't need to pack no gun. Everybody loved him."

She set the wineglass on the table in front of him. Desiree was a good woman. She cooked and cleaned like it was a paying job, never held out on sex and wasn't saddled with any kids. But the mouth. She never knew when to shut up.

"If people see me with you," she continued to rant, "they're gonna start hating on me too."

Littlefield reached for the wineglass. "I got a twenty thousand dollar retainer for taking the case," he said quietly.

Desiree's jaw dropped.

"I had planned to give you some of the money. But seeing how you feel . . ." He let his words linger in the air. "And I was hoping to finally get around to taking you on that trip to Jamaica like I promised."

Desiree sauntered over and held up the ice pack for him. "You're the lawyer, not me," she said, all sweetness now. "I'm sure you've got a good reason for representing that cop, so I'm just gonna have to stand by my man."

Littlefield took a sip of wine. "And I'm gonna stand by mine too," he said under his breath.

Just before noon the next day, Littlefield stood at the intersection of Jefferson and University Avenue, with a row of crimson and gold flowers in the foreground and a University of Southern California banner just over his shoulder. He thought about the men who had taken him for a ride the night before, and realized that they could easily pick him off from where he stood. The .38 strapped to his ankle eased some of that concern.

The number of reporters who had shown up for his impromptu press briefing wasn't nearly as large as the previous crowd, but was still a respectable showing nonetheless.

"I'm here to announce a $2,500 reward for anyone who may have witnessed the shooting of Deon Jackson," he said. "I believe my client, Officer Harold McIntyre, is the victim of a setup. It's our hope that someone out there saw what really happened that night. If you did, please call me." He rattled off his number.

After responding to a few questions with non-answers, Littlefield left. He had almost made it to his car when Gus Washington caught up with him.

"Man, what are you doing?" asked Washington. "You don't really believe this cover-up stuff, do you?"

Littlefield and Washington went way back. Whenever Littlefield wanted some positive press for one of his cases, he could count on the *Sentinel*. He opened his car door. "Actually, I do believe it."

The reporter chuckled. "So who's behind it?" Washington was a good reporter. Good enough to be at a prestigious paper like the *Times*. But he was far more committed to the community than to his bank account.

Littlefield wasn't sure how much he should reveal. "Most likely the University or somebody connected with 'em."

"And what makes you think that?"

"A number of things." Littlefield told him about the autopsy report and took out the note and the shards of glass. But Washington didn't react until Littlefield pointed to the bruise below his left eye and explained how he got it.

"Let's go get a bite to eat," Washington said. "On me."

Seven hours later, Littlefield was sitting in a dive bar near Manchester and La Brea, anxiously inspecting every white person who walked through the door. The man he was about to meet claimed to have information that would blow the Jackson shooting wide open. His call had come just minutes after Littlefield returned from his lunch meeting with Washington.

When the man, who called himself Brent, finally walked into the bar, he barely looked old enough to drive. And he wasn't white. He just sounded like it.

"So tell me what you know," Littlefield said, the minute Brent slid into the booth across from him. He had a short Afro and wore faded jeans and a UCLA T-shirt.

"There's something we need to get straight first," Brent said. His eyes bounced around the bar every few seconds.   Littlefield knew what Brent wanted to hear. "If you've got some useful information about the Jackson shooting, then the reward money's yours," he said.

"Man, I got plenty cash." Brent acted as if Littlefield had just insulted him. "I don't need money. I need legal representation."

"For what?"

"If what I have to say gets out, I could be facing some very serious charges. I'll tell you what I know, but only if you agree to represent me—free of charge."

"Okay," Littlefield said, not sure he would keep his word. "But only if the information's good enough. So what *do* you know?"

"Let's just say I do a little dealing and Deon Jackson was one of my biggest clients."

Littlefield felt his neck muscles constrict. "For how long?"

"A couple of years."

"Did anybody at the University know about it?"

"I don't think so."

Littlefield smiled. "So Deon Jackson had a cocaine problem."

"Man, I don't mess around with that stuff," Brent said, offended again.

Littlefield clasped his hands on the table. The kid was definitely beginning to annoy him. "So what do you sell?" he asked.

Brent proudly stuck out his chest and cocked his head to the side. "The best of the best. THG, Nandrolone, and Depo-Testosterone."

Littlefield's face went blank.

"C'mon, man," Brent said, "you must've been hiding under a rock or something. I sell the kind of drugs that can make a running back like Deon Jackson look like he's sailing across the sky. I sell designer steroids."

It took some doing, but Littlefield convinced Brent to repeat his story for Gus Washington. The three of them didn't leave the bar until close to midnight.

Brent admitted that he had been with Deon in Exposition Park the night Officer McIntyre pulled up. He also backed up McIntyre's story that Deon ran toward the campus, while Brent took off into the park. He didn't actually see the shooting, but by the time he had finished telling them everything he knew, including the particulars of his steroid sales to players at other colleges and a couple in the pros, Washington knew he had the story of the year.

When the *Sentinel* hit the street three days later, the story told a different version of the Deon Jackson shooting. Washington's report, which quoted an anonymous source and included the information Littlefield had provided, raised enough questions to give credence to Officer McIntyre's version of the shooting. The whereabouts of Deon Jackson's gun was still a mystery, but the combined weight of the evidence convinced even the most skeptical reader that the University might actually have disposed of it.

Littlefield came out smelling like a garden full of roses. One newspaper profiled him under the headline, The *Attorney Who Wasn't Blinded by Race*. When Shana Banks called the next day requesting a meeting with Littlefield and his client, he knew his press coverage was about to get even better.

When McIntyre spotted Littlefield walking up the steps of the D.A.'s office, the officer ran over and slapped him on the back. "I knew I hired the right attorney!" he grinned.

McIntyre's gratitude warmed Littlefield inside. "Let's go resolve this thing."

After passing through the metal detectors, they rushed up to Shana Bank's office, where they were immediately shown into a conference room. This one had expensive mahogany paneling, a long executive table and a decent view of downtown Los Angeles.

When Shana walked in, Littlefield had to force himself to concentrate on the case. She was wearing a slim-fitting skirt that nicely accentuated her rear end.

"Thanks for coming," she said, taking a seat opposite them. "I'm not sure where to begin." She turned to Officer McIntyre. "It appears that the media reports are correct. We got the autopsy report this morning and it showed steroids in Jackson's system."

Littlefield grinned at his client.

"In light of that, we're reexamining your version of what happened that night. We're also looking more closely into your allegation that the USC campus police confiscated Jackson's gun."

She paused. "I'd personally like to say I'm sorry you had to go through all of this. I understand the dangers police officers face every time they put on their uniforms. But we had no choice but to act upon the evidence we had at the time."

This woman was one class act, Littlefield thought. Hearing a D.A. admit to screwing up was like hearing God say He should've created Eve before Adam.

His cell phone rang.

"Excuse me," Littlefield said to Shana as he flipped his phone open and walked over to a corner of the room for privacy. He had promised Washington an exclusive on his meeting with Shana and assumed it was him calling now. But when he answered, he heard Brent's voice.

"There's something I forget to mention," Brent said. "I don't know if it's important or not, but I figured I should tell you."

Littlefield started to put him off, but something told him not to. He motioned to Shana. "I need to step outside to handle this call," he said. "I wouldn't normally leave my client alone with a D.A., but I figure he's safe with you."

Shana smiled and waved him off.

Littlefield stepped into the hallway and listened to what Brent had to say. The kid's words took a few seconds to register in Littlefield's brain, but when they did, rage mounted in his chest. He snapped his phone close and walked back into the room.

"I'd like to speak to my client," he said, his voice low and controlled. "Alone."

Shana started to say something, but saw the fury in Littlefield's eyes and hurried out of the room. Littlefield sat down across from McIntyre and glared at him. "You must really take me for a chump."

McIntyre's forehead creased in confusion. "Excuse me?"

"I have to give it to you," Littlefield continued, "your whole setup was actually pretty clever. You killed an unarmed man, then made it look like *you* were the victim."

McIntyre's neck began to redden. "What're you talking about? I didn't—"

"Cut the bullshit!" Littlefield shouted. "That call I just got was from the guy who was with Deon the night of the shooting. Jackson was only shot once, but the guy heard two gunshots. And the second one was followed by the sound of breaking glass."

McIntyre swallowed, but didn't speak.

"You shot out that streetlight, didn't you?" Littlefield spat. "And you're also the one who sent me that anonymous note. You deserve a damn Academy Award." All this time, Littlefield thought he had been using McIntyre, when the man had been scamming him. "The *Times* said your gun had only been fired once. So how'd you do it?"

A trace of a smile formed on McIntyre's lips. "Smart cops always carry their own personal weapon."

"So were those your buddies who kidnapped me outside my apartment?"

McIntyre's thin lips widened into a full smile, but he did not respond to the question.

"And I guess nobody's going to find Jackson's gun, because he didn't have one, right?" Littlefield massaged his temples.

This time, McIntyre nodded. "For what it's worth, the shooting *was* an accident. I still don't remember pulling the trigger. That should ease your conscience a bit."

The lack of remorse in McIntyre's voice sickened Littlefield. "My conscience is not what you should be worried about." He pushed his chair back from the table.

"Hey!" McIntyre shouted. "Where are you going?"

"You need to get yourself a new attorney. I quit."

Officer McIntyre leaned menacingly toward Littlefield, his palms flat on the table. "I paid you twenty thousand dollars. You can't quit."

"I can and I have. And, by the way, I think the real story of what happened to Deon Jackson is going to make a pretty interesting news story."

"Everything we've just discussed is protected by the attorney-client privilege." McIntyre's statement sounded like a threat.

"True," Littlefield replied. "But my other client, the steroid salesman, just might decide to cut a deal."

"That's not going to happen," McIntyre said slowly. "Because your little anonymous source is going to stay that way."

"Maybe, maybe not." Littlefield cracked a sly smile. "Perhaps somebody'll send the D.A. a note with his name and number, telling her to check the glass."

McIntyre suddenly dove across the table and grabbed Littlefield by the neck, slamming him hard against the wall. Littlefield tugged at McIntyre's wrists and tried to pry his hands loose, but the officer was larger and stronger. Just as Littlefield thought he was going to pass out, he managed to stomp down hard on McIntyre's instep.

The officer loosened his grip only slightly, giving Littlefield just enough time to catch a breath and drive his forehead against the bridge of the officer's nose. When McIntyre yelped in pain, Littlefield kneed him in the groin for good measure.

Shana rushed into the room. "What's going on in here?" She looked from a disheveled Littlefield to Officer McIntyre, rolled up in a ball on the floor.

"Actually, everything's just fine, Ms. Banks," Littlefield said, rubbing his throat and smiling down at McIntyre. "But we're going to have to postpone this meeting to give my former client a chance to find himself a new flunky."

*If we were to classify any of L.A.'s beach communities as landmarks then the eclectic town of **Venice** would top the list. Best known for its famous boardwalk where people soak in the funky atmosphere along with the SoCal sun, Venice also boasts a watery landmark--the Venice Canals.*

Conceived as one man's dream to mimic Venice, Italy, the canals date back over one hundred years, when twenty miles of interconnecting waterways and homes were built in 1904. The automobile's popularity doomed the unique neighborhood and by 1929, many of the canals were filled in and converted to roads. Today, only a few miles of the original canals remain but after decades of decay, the landmark neighborhood has experienced a renaissance, built on skyrocketing home prices. What was once home to beatniks, hippies, and artists in the 60's, has turned into a chic, exclusive L.A. address.

However, as you drift lazily down the restored canals in a private canoe, past multi-million dollar homes with landscaped walkways, take a deeper look beyond the peaceful pastoral. Something else lurks in the Venice Canals. A little thing called murder...

RUNNING VENICE
by A.H. Ream

"Alberto, you have to listen to me. Next time, it could be your finger Santos hacks off." I pressed the cell phone closer to my cheek, grinding it against my earring. "What would your family do then, Alberto? How would they pay for the doctors?"

Strip malls were giving way to hotels and palm trees as my car crept through traffic, inching west on Washington. I checked my rearview again. The cruiser had slid in behind me on the 405 and stayed two cars back ever since. Exiting when I exited. Turning when I turned. Slowing when I slowed. Even in the dark, I could see the top of his light bar peeking over the roof of the car behind me. Shit. Ticket-phobia was keeping me within shouting distance of the speed limit, and I was already late.

"*Se me hace que ya sé que tengo y no creo que haya Doctor pa' eso,*" Alberto whispered into the phone. *Maybe what happens to me, I don't need a doctor.*

I could see him, calloused hand cupped over the receiver so his wife and kids wouldn't hear. Five people in a one bedroom apartment with a toilet that mostly didn't work.

"*Oigo cosas feas, bien malas.*" *I hear bad things.*

I merged into the right lane, taking my foot off the gas and squinting at the street signs. Angry drivers tried to squeeze between my side mirror and the next lane of traffic, honking and giving me the finger along the way.

"What bad things, Alberto? ¿Pos que oyes?"

No answer.

I tucked the cell phone against my shoulder, grabbed a street map off the passenger seat and shook it open. It unfurled like a giant tarp, covering my steering wheel.

"Alberto?"

I turned right off Washington, sliding into the residential heart of Venice, the sometimes-funky, sometimes-seedy, redheaded stepchild of L.A.'s beachside neighborhoods.

"Alberto?" I said again.

There was a click and then silence.

"Shit." I looked at the little glowing screen. Call ended, it said, low battery. I told it what it could do with its battery and shoved the damned thing in my pocket. I double-parked on the one-way street and kept an eye on my mirror. The cruiser slid by in slow motion but stayed on Washington.

I reached over the *mapus giganticus* and snatched up my notebook, flipping through the pages for Manuel Santos's address.

Roger, my news editor, had listened to my progress report that morning in his office. "I think it's time to go see him in person," he said.

"It's too early," I told him. "Alberto's all I've got on the record. If I tip my hand now, every source in three counties will dry up."

"You either go see him today or not at all. It's a non-story as it is." He leaned back in his chair. "Come up with something now or drop it for good."

Roger had been trying to push me off the Santos story for weeks, denying overtime requests and filling my days with city council meetings and weather stories. I was—without a doubt—being punished. He'd said, "Let's have a drink some time." I'd said I didn't drink with married men. And now he was tearing the story out of my hands—my best story—the kind that filled an office with little gold plaques and statues, the kind that moved you up from reporter to editor. It was sabotage. He was sending me in unprepared. Guaranteed failure.

"Right," I said through gnashed teeth. "Today then."

I went back to my desk and plowed through every note, every source, every statistic, anything I could find. I was training for the interview like it was a boxing match at my daddy's gym. Head down, eye on the bag. Work now. Kill Roger later.

I flipped through my notebook. Santos had immigrated twenty years before. He started his business putting up fences in Beverly Hills and graduated to constructing government buildings and commercial property. That and abusing the illegals he hired to do the heavy lifting. It had been an open secret for a while, but the rumors were getting louder and scarier. He'd cut off the ring finger of a man asking for time off to care for his sick wife. No ring, no marriage, no problem. And no leaks. Santos's employees were more afraid of the INS than of him. Until Alberto.

That afternoon, I called Manuel Santos and introduced myself. "Samantha Martinez, calling from the

Herald-Star," I said after I'd been transferred from the receptionist to the secretary and finally to Santos. "I'm doing a piece on your business. I'd like a few minutes of your time for some questions."

"Today, I am busy," he said. "Tonight you'll come see me at my house. 2825 Austin Street, Venice. Ten o'clock."

It was 10:05, and I was still double-parked, squinting at the tiny blue roads snaking around the canals on my map. Dug a hundred years ago in a flurry of madness and grandeur, the fingers of water spread out from a central channel like a line drawing of a toothbrush. Bridges crisscrossed at unpredictable intervals, some open to cars, some not. Streets ended and started and narrowed with all the forethought and planning God gave a drunken monkey.

I was staring at the map and never saw it coming. My head slammed into the side window. Pain spread across my forehead, reaching down my face to the bridge of my nose. My car was cattywampus in the road, pointing at an angle toward the other side of the street. The rosary looped around my rearview mirror was swaying back and forth like a hypnotist's pocket watch. I turned to look behind me. The front end of the cruiser was buried in my passenger-side rear fender. The two of us made a V sitting sideways in the road.

I opened my door and stumbled out, my hand to my head. The point of impact felt hot, like all the blood in my body was rushing to form a knot as quickly as possible. I looked down at my fingers, trying to see if any had leaked out.

"Hands up, Sam."

The officer was now out of his car, too.

"What?" I was starting to feel dizzy, and none of this was making any sense.

"Hands up." Matter of fact and quiet. Just loud enough to travel from him to me.

In the dark, the outline of his body was nothing but a black shadow. But even so, I was pretty damn sure there was gun pointed at my chest. I put my hands up.

"What the hell's going on?!" I yelled. "Do I know you?"

"Shut up." Too quiet, like he didn't want anyone else to hear.

Something in the base of my skull started to vibrate.

He walked around the tail end of his car, advancing across the center of the V, gun raised. The closer he got, the better I could see. The badge on his chest, the name tag. Kraus. Every story I'd ever written was speeding through my head like a microfiche machine on fast forward. Searching. Searching. Kraus...Kraus...I couldn't place it. I didn't know a Kraus, hadn't interviewed a Kraus. Jesus Christ, what had I done to this guy? He was getting close to the nose of my car, close to me. I lowered my hands.

"Hands up."

"Am I under arrest?" I asked.

"Sure," he said. "Why not?"

Adrenaline was leaking into my system, speeding up my heart rate and tightening my muscles.

"For what?" I asked.

"I'll think of something."

"Someone's going to report the accident," I said.

He laughed. Not hard, but a chuckle. "Why?" he asked. "An accident involving a cop car? Who would they call? The police? A bit redundant, isn't it?" The yards between us had become just a few feet. "Now, you and I are going for a ride."

He reached to his belt and pulled loose a set of cuffs. He held one bracelet in his hand, and I watched as the other twisted and dangled, catching the glow from my headlights. Flash, twist, flash, twist.

I turned and took off down the street. At first there was nothing. No sound at all, and I pictured him staring down the sight of his gun. I listened for the crack, braced for the pain. But it didn't come. I had bet if he didn't want to shout, he didn't want to let off a shot either. Wouldn't want the neighbors to hear that. So there was nothing, nothing but the pounding footsteps starting up behind me.

My brain was desperately searching for the logic. What was the story here, and how could I get it without getting shot? I picked up the mantra in time with my stride. Get story. Don't die. Get story. Don't die. Not necessarily in that order.

I cut right, running parallel to the canal. The water was still and black. Even the little rowboats tied up in front of each house were motionless. I picked up speed, my loafers smacking against the sidewalk. The canal made a sharp left, and I followed it. The footsteps were still behind me, steady—slap, slap, slap—but slower than mine. I was two houses past the bend when I looked over my shoulder. He hadn't made the turn yet, and I was out of his sight line. Arms out, I dived over a short hedge that separated one of the houses from the sidewalk.

I lay face down in the grass, feeling the cold earth under my belly and breathing in the fishy smell of the water three feet away. I reached in my pocket for my cell phone, keeping low and close to the hedge. Who should I call? The police? And tell them what? One of their boys was crazier than a shithouse rat? Get the story. Don't die. Get the story. Don't die. I dialed by touch in the dark.

"*Herald-Star* copy desk. Janice speaking."

I prayed he'd still be there.

"Get me Roger," I said, trying to keep my voice low.

"What? Who is this?"

"Get me Roger," I whispered again. "It's an emergency."

The sound of footsteps had stopped. Had he turned back? Given up? Moved on to some other hapless woman stuck on the side of the road?

"Look, ma'am, I don't think I can help you. If you'll call back tomorrow..."

"Sam Martinez," I whispered a little louder. "This is Sam Martinez. Get me Roger."

"Oh, Sam. Sorry. Couldn't hear you very well. I'll..."

The phone went dead. I pulled it off my ear and stared at the display. Battery dead.

"Good hiding place."

I could see his boots through the base of the hedge.

"Roll over, nice and slow."

But damned if I wasn't feeling uncooperative. I dropped my cell phone in the dirt and pressed up off the ground with both hands. I was halfway to my feet when the mist hit the back of my head. I could feel it cold and wet, like hair spray straight out of the aerosol. My neck was on fire. I turned to the side.

Shhhhh.

Another squirt. The left side of my face took the brunt of it. I couldn't breathe. I stumbled forward, holding my cheek. His hand gripped the back of my shirt. Wadding it up in his fist and pulling the fabric tight around my windpipe, he yanked me over the bushes, dragging me through the sharp branches and thorns.

"Stop!" I screamed, then remembered something from a self-defense class. "Fire!" I yelled. "Fire! Fire!"

Shhhhh.

The pepper spray went straight into my mouth. I choked and spat and started to vomit. He still had hold of my shirt, and he was pulling me backward. I stumbled, falling on my butt. My eyes were streaming and burning, and I couldn't see. He shoved something in my mouth, something soft. Fabric. It was soaking up the vomit that was still pooled on my tongue. I tried to spit it out. He pulled tighter on my shirt, cutting off my air. I gasped, sucking the gag in deeper. He clamped his hand, now in a leather glove, over my face and shoved me onto my stomach. He had a knee in my spine and a hand pulling my head back until I thought it would snap. I felt the metal bracelet go over one wrist. He let go of my head to fasten the other, then yanked me up onto my knees by my tethered hands.

I did the only thing I could. I twisted and flailed and fought. He pulled me to my feet, my back to him, dragging me the way we'd come. I kicked out, trying to build up momentum, to pitch myself forward as he yanked my arms backward. My shoulders screamed. The fabric was lodged so far into my mouth my chest was heaving, my throat tightening, my gag reflex on full alert. I tried to suck as much air as I could through my nose. Don't die. Don't die. Don't die.

I was losing ground. I kicked out again, high and hard, with everything I had left.

My foot exploded. I could feel the fractures spreading through bone like a fault line. The huge concrete urn I'd connected with, the one balanced on the edge of a low stone wall, teetered for a moment before falling onto the sidewalk. The only thing louder than the crash was the barking. The falling urn woke up every dog on the block. Deep throaty barks and high yippy ones, first just a few and then spreading outward like a mushroom cloud until every dog in Venice was howling. Bedroom lights started flicking on, little squares of yellow light popping to life up and down the canal, reflecting into the black water until its surface was spotted with wobbling reflections.

The crippling pain in my foot brought me down, butt first, onto the sidewalk. Tears poured down my face, my whimpers muffled deep in my throat behind the vomit-soaked gag. The cop leaned over me, so close I could smell his aftershave. Cradling me like a baby, he lifted me off the sidewalk and walked quickly in the opposite direction from his car.

I started to squirm, tried to loosen his grip. He leaned to the right, dropping his shoulder so my legs hung down just a foot or so off the ground. He veered closer to the mismatched fences lining each yard. Closer. I squirmed harder. Closer. My fractured foot bumped against the first rail in a wrought iron fence. Then the next. Then the next. My foot slapped against rail after rail, sounding like a boxer working the speed bag. My chest heaved as each sob got louder and stronger. I stopped squirming, no longer able to think past the pain, past the spider's web of breaks lacing around the tiny bones in my foot.

He turned right at the next cross street, stepped easily over the low fence surrounding the corner house and dropped me next to the metal and glass door. He pulled a ring of keys from his pocket and started flipping through them. The house was a concrete box, modern and cold, more suited to a law office than a home. But expensive. Two million, three maybe.

He found whatever key he needed. I heard it slide into the lock. A high-pitched beep sounded. He punched some buttons to stop the beeping, picked me up, carried me across the threshold and dropped me in the middle of the floor.

The room was absolutely dark. I felt a rug soft under my cheek but couldn't make out even the vaguest shadow of furniture against the blackness. Kraus' shoes, muffled on the carpet, started to click as he moved farther away. Tile, maybe? There was a pause and a rustle of fabric, the squishing sound of a cushion compressing and then nothing. We were waiting.

My cheeks were wet with tears and pepper spray. Snot was running out of my nose. It occurred to me that I might die. That this might be the last house I would ever be in. The last rug I'd ever touch. The last man I'd ever see. Self-pity rose up out of my chest and made a lump the size of a walnut in my windpipe. I thought about my sister. She was going to have the baby in a month, and I wasn't going to be an aunt. I wasn't going to finish planning the baby shower or hold her hand in the delivery room. I thought about my mother, saw her in her best Sunday dress kneeling down to pray between the pews. And I prayed with her.

There was a rumble from deep inside the house, gears turning, metal on metal as a garage door somewhere slowly started to lift. A car engine. The opening and closing of a car door. An interior door opening, footsteps and the click of a light switch. Hidden fixtures sent out soft beams from recessed niches and behind potted palms. Kraus was sitting, legs crossed, on a tropical print couch.

"This was not the plan."

It was the voice that had given me a time and address that afternoon, heavy with the same accent my father and mother had carried their whole lives.

"She ran," Kraus said. "She made a scene."

"So you bring her to my house? You bring her here and drop her like stinky garbage on my rug?"

I wondered which of his tripwires I'd hit. Maybe when I'd requested copies of the city's building contracts? Some secretary, some copy room boy with a debt to pay? Was it one of the subcontractors I'd called? An electrician? A plumber? What was Roger's folksy wisdom? Spook one cow, spook the herd.

I could hear Kraus's boots on the tile again. He was standing. *Click. Click.* Coming closer.

Santos kept talking. "I pay you. I pay you and your partner and many, many others. I pay, and I expect service. I get what I pay for from the others. Why do you fail me?"

Santos stepped over me and into my line of vision. He reached up and ran his thumb along Kraus's jaw. "Why?"

"I didn't fail." Kraus's voice was softer. "I'm just not finished yet."

"You bring her to my house," Santos gestured to me. "This problem was supposed to go away. Poof. Gone. But it's not gone. It's in my living room. It's stinking up my rug."

Kraus reached for his gun.

Smack.

It was so quick I blinked, unsure if I'd seen it. Kraus's face was twisted to the side, just where Santos's slap had left it.

"You are stupid," Santos hissed. "You are a stupid, stupid boy. And I don't like stupid boys. You shoot her here, you make a big noise. Maybe somebody makes a report. Makes for me more cops I have to pay. Makes a mess. Leaves evidence. You stick to the plan, take her out of the city like I say before. You take her to the mountains, take her past where the hikers go, no one knows." Santos ran his hand over the cop's face where a red hand print was starting to show. "You make Papa happy, huh." He patted his cheek.

"Let me borrow your car," Kraus said, still looking to the side, not bringing his face around to Santos. "Mine's too far away. She'll attract attention. I'll put her in the trunk, drive her out there tonight."

"My trunk is..." Santos flitted his hand in the air like he was searching for the right word, "full."

"Full of what?" Kraus brought his eyes around to face him, anger starting to work at his jaw.

"An inconvenience."

Santos reached up to touch his face, but Kraus pulled back. Stepping around Santos, he pulled the ring of keys from his pocket, crossed the room in three steps and scooped me up again. We were moving quickly through the foyer, the dining room, the kitchen, through the door I'd heard open earlier and into a small, one-car garage. Santos had left the door raised, and I could smell the briny canals just a few feet away.

Without putting me down, Kraus fiddled with the keys, found the right one and slid it into the trunk's lock. The lid rose slowly. I tried to scream, tried to scream through the vomit and the gag and the pain. Kraus moved his hand from my shoulder to my throat and squeezed, choking off my muffled noises and my air.

Alberto's body was curled up, knees to chin, in the trunk. His calloused hands lay limp and useless by his face. His eyes were open, and his jaw was hanging slack.

"What the f —" Kraus stared into the trunk, his grip loosening.

He'd let his guard down. I twisted to the right and dug my hand into his groin. I grabbed hold and crushed him between my fingers with everything I had. He let out a strangled whimper and doubled over, dropping me on the slick concrete floor. I rolled over onto my knees and pushed up to stand. The weight on my broken foot brought bile into the back of my throat. Forcing myself to swallow it down, I stumbled, crippled, toward the smell of the canal.

I felt primal. Fight or flight. Adrenaline pulsing through my system, more and more with every step until my skin tingled with it, until it deadened the pain and made me feel dizzy and lightheaded. I pulled air through my nose, willing it into my lungs, steadying my brain. I heard the cop curse behind me, heard him call for Santos, heard him stagger to his feet. But I didn't turn. Didn't look back. I was slow at first, limping. I heard Kraus behind me, his footsteps uneven, probably still cradling his bruised testicles in his hand. I worked the gag as I ran, pushing at it with my tongue, opening and closing my jaw, working it loose. Faster, faster. Stabbing at it with my tongue, more and more until it fell. I sucked a deep breath through my mouth and started to cough. I picked up the pace, let my smashed foot take a little more weight. I was running. My gait was wild and jerky, but I was running.

Slap. Slap.

Kraus was still behind me. He was yelling, but not at me. I didn't pay attention to the words, just kept pushing. Harder, faster. My arms dangling behind me. I made a hard right at the canal and ran along its edge, pushing farther into the tangle of waterways and mismatched houses.

Slap. Slap.

I cranked left, stumbling on the uneven boards of the foot bridge that arched high and steep across the water. My toe caught in one of the cracks, and I pitched forward face first, landing hard. The sudden slam forced the air out of my chest in a whoosh. My brain was panicking. Air. Air. I tried to suck it back in, tried to inflate my lungs.

I raised up onto my knees and looked over the crest of the bridge. At the bottom was Santos. His stance was wide and unmoving, waiting for me to come to him. I struggled to my feet and whipped around, back the way I'd come.

Slap. Slap. Slap.

Kraus had made his way to the bridge, too, blocking off my exit, his sidearm pointed at my chest. I heard a loud crack and saw the flash. The air next to my ear whistled. So much for quiet. I spun on my good heel. Another crack. Pain like a lightning strike stabbed through my shoulder.

I made a running leap at the side of the bridge, letting the guard rail hit me square in the stomach and using the momentum to pitch myself over. I went down hard, back first, and was swallowed by the frigid canal. I let myself sink, feeling the water brush across my body like a thousand fingers. I bumped gently against the rocky bottom. It was only four feet down, but in the night, under the black water, I was invisible. Blood oozed from my shoulder, floated up and dissipated like smoke. There was a pop and a whish from somewhere above me and then another, as Kraus fired blindly into the canal.

Staying close to the bottom, I spun around, face down and started to dolphin kick, undulating my body with the movement of the water, feeling my thighs tighten and then relax as the rhythm caught hold. My arms lay heavy on my back, resting against my spine. Kick. Undulate. Kick. Undulate. I closed my eyes and let the current tickle my lashes, let my brain relax. Kick. Undulate. Kick. Undulate.

I broke the surface for air. I was too far away, and it was too dark for Kraus to be accurate. I didn't bother to turn when I heard another shot. I just sucked the fishy smell into my lungs and sank back down. Kick. Undulate. Kick. Undulate.

My canal made a hard right up ahead, and I followed it, trying to remember the map I'd had spread out over my steering wheel half an hour earlier. I pictured the toothbrush. I knew I was on one of the bristles and the handle was somewhere up ahead stretching to the left, back toward Washington Boulevard and traffic and safety in numbers. I took another breath and saw the water coming to a *T* not more than a hundred feet ahead. I went back under and made a left turn at the cross. Without my arms, my swim was slow, and my legs started to cramp.

Traffic rumbled overhead; a horn honked. Washington was right above me. I was taking more breaths and hugging the side. I came up for air one last time and stayed up, treading water. My chest bumped the huge concrete drainage pipe sticking out of the bank. A plastic cup floated in front of my face, and a half dozen drunken pedestrians were crossing the sidewalk ten feet above me.

"Hey!" I yelled, competing with the car engines and the canned mariachi music pouring out of the Mexican restaurant nearby. "Hey!"

A blonde in a tiny tank top looked over her shoulder. "Ohmigod!" she yelled back. "Ohmigod, there's somebody down there!"

All three of the men stumbled toward the edge of the water. They lifted me up by my shoulders, and one of them whispered about the cuffs. But I was too exhausted, too hurt, too scared to care. I screamed when they tried to stand me up. The numbing effects of the adrenaline were gone, and the pain in my foot was blinding. They carried me up the side and deposited me on the pavement.

Tank-top girl pulled a cell phone from her pocket and started to dial.

"No police," I choked. "No police."

The group exchanged looks.

"Let me call my husband first."

I gave the newsroom number to the girl, who dialed and held the receiver up to my ear.

"Honey," I said, when Roger picked up, "it's Sam. There's been an accident. Come get me. Corner of Washington and Pacific."

The group waited with me, camped out on the sidewalk and blocking foot traffic. A few drivers stared, but no one stopped. One of the men took off his button-down shirt and tied it around my shoulder. It was still oozing blood, but the bullet had just grazed it, leaving nothing more than a bad cut.

Roger pulled up against the curb, blocking his lane and sending up a riot of honking horns. The group deposited me in the passenger seat and dispersed.

I sat there, dripping and bleeding on his leather seats.

"Jesus, you want to go to the hospital?"

The smell of dashboard sealant and new carpet was nauseating.

"I've got something I have to do first. Fourth and St. Michael Street, Boyle Heights." As an afterthought, "Please."

Boyle Heights was a mile and a half east of downtown. It had been the starting point for a dozen different immigrant groups since the early 1900s: Russians, Jews, Japanese, Mexicans. Mostly Mexican now. And up until very recently, the home of Alberto Cruz. Instinctively, my right hand tried to make the sign of the cross but only managed to make the cuffs jingle.

Roger was merging onto the 405, making his way toward the 10 and downtown. He glanced over at the sound of my musical wristwear. "Maybe we should call the police."

"The cops and I aren't on very good terms."

"Sam..."

"Boyle Heights," I repeated. "Fourth and St. Michael."

He faced front and concentrated on negotiating traffic. I watched him watch the taillights in front of us.

"You didn't ask me what happened."

"Huh?" He glanced in my direction like he hadn't heard me, a bluff that wouldn't have worked at the most amateur of poker tables. He coughed and tried to recover himself. "I figured, you know, you'll tell me when you're ready."

"Your patience is impressive."

He shrugged.

"Manuel Santos's patience is impressive, too. He finds out some meddlesome reporter's gonna blow his business all to hell, he just waits for her to call him up for an interview."

Roger cleared his throat. "You're not making any sense, Sam."

"Must be the head wound."

"I'm gonna call my wife. Tell her I'm gonna be awhile."

I watched him dial. Funny not to have his wife's number programmed into his cell phone.

"Hey, honey," he said. "It's Roger. I'm with Sam." He paused. "Uh huh. She's right here next to me. There's been some sort of accident, and she needs to go to Boyle Heights. So I'm going to be a little late." He paused. "Oh, it shouldn't be too long. We're going there now. Fourth and St. Michael." Another pause. "Okay, sweetie, talk to you soon."

I held my tongue on the 10, watching the sloping mountain of downtown buildings rise up, peak and fall off again. Roger checked his rearview mirror sixteen times. I kept count. We crossed the L.A. River and swung left where the 5 and the 10 merge. In the daylight, I could've seen the apartment my parents had lived in thirty years before.

I broke the silence. "Nice car. New?"

"What?" His face looked flushed, like he was about to start sweating. "Oh, yeah. It's new." He glanced in the rearview again while I studied the logo in the middle of the steering wheel.

"Expensive."

"It's, uh, it's one of the low-end ones."

He exited onto Fourth Street, passing row after row of groceries and restaurants and furniture repair shops painted with bright murals. Even at night under the muddying yellow haze of the street lamps, the pinks and reds and greens were glaring. We passed the bakery my mother had walked to on Sunday mornings. I'd stand next to her clutching her leg while she spoke in rapid Spanish to the counter girl. Someday this is where we'll get your wedding cake, she told me every week, a big one with yellow roses all over.

Roger turned left onto St. Michael. He pulled the fancy car up against the curb, checked the rearview again, frowned, and turned around to look behind him.

"Expecting someone?" I asked.

"Huh? No. I was just, you know, being careful. I, uh, heard this area was high crime."

I stayed silent, letting my jaw work itself back and forth.

"Car thefts, muggings, assaults."

Silence.

"You should, uh, be careful around here. Dangerous."

"Well, maybe you should wait here," I said. "Just in case any of those car thieves happen by."

I watched his entire frame relax. "Good idea. I'll stay here."

Roger had to reach over me to open the car door. I bumped it closed with my butt, brushing off his half-hearted offers of more help. I took a deep, ragged breath, put as much weight as I dared on my left foot and hobbled across the sidewalk. The building was electric pink stucco and shaped like a giant *C*. The entrance to the center courtyard was blocked by a rusting wrought iron fence. I checked the list of tenants, turned around and used my cuffed hands to press the button marked "Cruz."

A soft voice crackled through the box. "*¿Quién es?*"

Alberto's wife.

"*Señora Cruz, déjeme entrar por favorcito, su márido me conoce. Es una emergencia.*" Please let me in. I'm a friend of your husband's. It's an emergency.

There was no danger of Roger overhearing. He spoke about as much Spanish as I did Hebrew.

"*Mi marido no está.*"

I leaned my forehead against the wall. He wasn't home, she'd said. I was suddenly very tired. "*Él no va a regresar,*" I told her. *He's not coming home.*

The intercom went silent.

"Rosa," I pleaded. "*Por favor, déjeme entrar.*"

There was a click, and the front gate unlatched. I turned my back to it again, this time to turn the knob.

The courtyard was paved and cracking. Chunks of concrete jutted up like mountain ranges, but someone had bothered to plant geraniums in little plastic pots and scatter them around the edges. The windows had bars, and behind the bars, bed sheets were hung as curtains. Somewhere a radio sang a love song in Spanish. The staircase was worn and cracking like the courtyard, but it had been recently swept. Under the bare light bulb, I could see the bristle marks in the dust. I leaned one hip against the wall and hopped slowly up the stairs, grimacing with each step.

At the top of the stairs, I used my elbow to knock on her door.

"*Eres valiente pero terca.*"

Santos's frame filled the doorway, and my stomach seized up. My already damp underwear got even wetter.

Brave, he called me, brave but predictable. Obviously very predictable. I felt stupid. Scared and stupid.

"Where's Rosa?" I asked, refusing to give Santos the comfort of his native tongue.

He grabbed my shackled arm and pulled me inside.

The room was small, hot and poorly lit. The counter, sink and hot plate that served as the kitchen were on my right, a pot of coffee burning on the plate. Rosa was on my left. She sat on a hand-me-down couch with the youngest of the three children on her lap. A little boy, Alberto had told me, Carlos. He couldn't have been more than two. Rosa was a smaller woman than I had pictured, short with a soft face and a belly heavy with a pregnancy Alberto hadn't mentioned. Her hair was still coal black even as the skin around her eyes had started to crinkle like crepe paper. She didn't look twice at my injuries, my wet clothes, the blood-soaked shirt tied to my shoulder. She just clasped her hands around her son.

"I don't understand."

"I imagine there are many things you do not understand." Santos turned and took the baby from Rosa's arms, holding him against his hip like he was his own. It was disgusting.

"My story isn't worth this. You'd lose your business, but this—me, Alberto—it doesn't make sense. It's too risky."

He held my stare but said nothing.

"There's something else."

Santos shrugged and patted the little boy's leg. Carlos had tears in his eyes and kept looking over his shoulder at his mother and sisters.

"You didn't cut that man's finger off because he wanted time with his wife, did you?"

Another shrug.

"What was he? A runner who came up short?"

"Terca pero no estúpida." Predictable, he said, but not stupid.

"You killed Alberto because he was running for you, too. Running and talking."

"Ah, but you're not as smart as you think. Is she, Rosa?"

Rosa was looking at her knees and clutching the hand of the daughter beside her, a girl maybe six years old. Rosa didn't look up, didn't answer.

"Give me the delivery," he said to her.

She reached up under her dress and pulled out a brick of white powder, wrapped in clear plastic and heavy-duty tape. She set it down on the worn rug in front of her feet, and then reached up her dress again. She took out another, and another, until her pregnant belly was flat.

"Coyotes don't come cheap," Santos said. "But I pay. I pay every cent. Not to bring over just one man, but a whole family." He clicked his tongue. "Very expensive. Rosa made a few runs, but all these babies..." He handed the boy back to his mother. "She was too slow. It was time for Alberto to do his part."

"And he wouldn't?"

"Alberto was a coward. A stupid coward."

Rosa clenched her knees but said nothing.

"He thinks he can get out of paying his family's debt by talking to a reporter?" He took a step closer to me. "He underestimates the man he is dealing with." Another step.

I backed up against the kitchen counter.

"Where's Kraus?" I asked.

Santos smiled. "Kraus and Roger are taking a little drive together." He was so close without the cuffs I could have reached out and touched him. "I think your newspaper may have an open position soon." I felt his breath on my face. "I think they may have two."

He grabbed my throat in his right hand, pushing his thumb into my larynx. I felt my eyes bulge, the counter dig into my arms still chained behind my back. I yanked at the cuffs, scratching at them, making gashes in my wrists. If I could only get them off, if I had my hands, I could fight him. I tried to twist, tried to kick. He sidestepped me, shoving his thumb deeper into my throat. I heard myself start to gurgle, choking and suffocating.

The couch creaked. But before he could turn, she was behind him. She shoved the six-inch kitchen knife straight into his back. He let go of my throat and stumbled backward. My windpipe felt like it had collapsed. He screamed and sank to his knees. I coughed and sputtered, watching the stain spread from the handle of the knife, the only part still visible, until his tailored white shirt looked like a Japanese flag. He opened his mouth again but nothing came out except a string of bloody drool. I hobbled to the other side of the room and stood next to Rosa. We stood shoulder to shoulder, waiting. Five minutes. Ten. Twenty.

When she was sure he was gone, she spoke. *"Váyanse a la cama, y se me quedan hay hasta que yo diga."*

Both girls obeyed and hurried out of the room, the oldest carrying Carlos in her arms.

My throat felt bruised; my voice was rough. *"¿Ustéd que haría?"*

"Hay un basurero en el callejón. Nadie se va a dar cuenta que ahi un poquito más de basura," she answered. *There is a trash bin in the alley. No one will notice a little extra garbage.*

Rosa fetched Alberto's toolbox, dragging it down the hall by the handle. Too heavy to lift, it was the size of a microwave with large metal handles dangling off either side. She unlatched the top and pulled out a hacksaw.

"Voltéate," she said.

I turned my back and listened to her cutting through the chain of my cuffs. With freed hands, I used the phone to call myself a cab and then hobbled as fast as my foot would take me out the door and down the stairs. I clutched the railing as I slid down the treads, two and three at a time. There wasn't enough air, not in that apartment, not even in the courtyard. I let myself out the gate and struggled up the sidewalk, putting as much distance as possible between that night and myself. I sat on the corner, my back pressed against a mural of the Virgin Mary painted on the front of a convenience store and waited for the cab to take me to the hospital.

I tried not to think about the hacksaw and how Rosa was going to make Santos small enough to carry down to the trash bin. I was desperate for anything to push the picture out of my mind.

I was halfway through saying my rosary, picturing the one that still hung in my car, when the cab stopped at the curb.

"Hail Mary, full of grace, the Lord is with thee..."

Before we leave the unique town of Venice, consider this: the next time you toss a stale bagel to a fat duck that's paddling down one of the Venice Canals, remember that dead ducks tell no tales...

SOME CREATURE I CARE ABOUT
by Arthur Coburn

Steve never knew exactly when the guy moved in. You couldn't see the next yard from Steve's place because the high chain-link fence between them had so much ivy on it that a squad of Turkish cavalry could have hidden behind it.

One day he heard grunting from behind the ivy when he was sitting on his deck overlooking the canal, trying to read an ancient history book: *The Assyrian Empire in All Its Splendor*. He liked the idea of reading it, but he couldn't do it very long without getting bored. He hadn't reached that point yet when he heard a man shout, "Fuck you! Leave me alone, you little shit."

Steve hated noisy neighbors. They were an insult to the perfect haven that he and his friends called the Canals. One side of Steve's house faced the alley—a drab strip of concrete arrayed with garbage cans—but the other side looked out on one of the few picturesque canals remaining from the huge complex that real estate developer Abbot Kinney had designed in the thirties, when he returned from the "real" Venice, in Italy, to California.

Fronting the canal was a sidewalk, over which branches of exotic trees and plants looped and curled like the feathers of huge tropical birds. Steve loved to wander canal-side, where reflections of sky and houses in the placid water were broken only by sunken canoes and kayaks, or by the families of ducks that considered the house dwellers intruders.

Steve's yard, enclosed by walls of bamboo and ivy, was an amazingly quiet refuge—his only visitors ducks and other birds, squirrels, neighborhood cats, and the odd possum. Irritated by the swearing from behind the fence, Steve rose from his chair, ready to tell off whoever was breaking the tranquil mood. He charged out his front gate and saw a frightened woman leading a three-year-old away from the opening to the next yard.

Steve approached the gate to his neighbor's house. He peered in and saw a beanpole-thin man about fifty, wearing a tattered suit and a fedora. The guy was bent forward, arranging a bedroll on the sea of ivy covering the front yard. He had sunken eyes like dark moon craters and heavy gray beard stubble. His hands were dirty and greasy. Steve smelled his body odor from ten feet away.

Steve didn't like homeless people so close to his house. Once he had strolled out to the canal to consider, for the hundredth time, the possibility of repairing the damaged canoe that had floated beside the bulkhead since Steve had rented the house six years before. Many of his friends used little boats to explore the canals. But Steve, still harboring the memory of a near-drowning at camp when he was seven, had never been able to bring himself either to swim in the Pacific Ocean, nor to venture out in the canoe.

On that umpteenth walk, he'd found a grizzled guy wrapped in a blanket sleeping in the canoe. Steve felt invaded. "This isn't a place you can stay," he said.

The guy hadn't uttered a word, just stared at him as if he'd heard so many dismissive voices that he couldn't react anymore. Steve retreated inside the house, but felt guilty. He went to the kitchen and returned with a dozen cans of tuna and soup. "I hope things go better for you," he said. The guy nodded, stepped out of the canoe and moved on.

This new invader was different. He was stomping down the ivy as if he owned the place, and with jerky, irritated swings of his bony arms, snorting as he arranged a couple of boxes beside his bedroll. Steve walked away. "My neighbor will get rid of him," he told himself.

But he remembered that he seldom saw his neighbor, whose name he thought was Hal. He'd once received a piece of the man's mail. When he'd knocked on Hal's front door, no one had answered. The guy was a reclusive character, reputed to have been a dog groomer before he retired. Hal might not walk out to his front yard for weeks. And the homeless guy might decide to settle in.

Steve made a point of making noise—clomping his feet across his deck. Then he decided to sing, meaning it to be a kind of musical pissing, to mark his territory. Maybe, he thought, the homeless guy would decide it wasn't a great place to stay. Steve picked an old hymn from his teenage years in church.

"He walks in the garden with me, while the dew is still on the roses. And the voice I hear falling on my ear, the Son of God disclo-o-ses."

"Shut the fuck up, asshole," the guy next door shouted. "Who the hell do you think you are?" The man had a grating nasal voice that seemed to rise in his throat from some deep angry place where only rusty, broken noises could survive.

"I *live* here." Steve's voice rose. "This is my house. So don't tell me when to sing or not."

"Shut up!"

"Who the hell do you think you are?"

"Shut the fuck up!"

"Listen, asshole, if you don't pipe down I'm gonna call the cops."

"Shut up!"

"You shut up."

"Shut up!"

"You!"

Steve saw himself in kindergarten, tugging with all his might against his friend, Teddy Pemrose, for possession of a metal fire engine. *It's mine. Is not. Is too. Is not.*

Steve went inside and dialed 911. But it occurred to him that if he called the cops and had the guy hauled away, he might just come back at night and put a brick through his windshield. He hung up, took a deep breath, and returned to the deck.

"Fuck you, shithead," the homeless guy shouted.

"Look, sorry about the bad start we had. Have a good day."

"Shut up!"

Steve lay back in his recliner and decided not to respond.

The guy kept trying. "Shut the fuck up. You piece of shit. Shut up."

Steve breathed deeply and closed his eyes.

Ten *shut ups* later, Steve went inside.

He met Marty when he took his Mercedes in for a new fuel pump.

In reality he didn't exactly "meet" her. She had been chatting with the mechanic, pointing to various parts of her car and acting out with her body what was going wrong. She was like a crackling fire, full of life and energy.

Steve noticed that her jeans had long streaks on them where the white threads were bared, like furrows in a field. And one of her thumbs was bandaged. Her car was an ancient 300SL with lots of dents. He wondered if she were a just a step or two from being homeless. He'd read about women who had been divorced and couldn't make their house payments. They would live in their cars and go to malls to freshen up during the day.

But she looked too cheerful for that, and when she smiled at the mechanic, Steve couldn't help smiling himself. Steve wanted to meet her, but it seemed too brash to just walk over and say, "Hi, will you give me your number?" When the mechanic left for a second, Steve hoped she'd look at him so he could smile. But she didn't.

When she and the mechanic walked to the far side of her car, Steve edged over to the computer screen on the counter and copied down her name and phone number.

He called her that night.

"Hello," she said.

"Marty?"

"Who's this?"

"It's Steve."

"I don't talk to telemarketers."

"I'm not a telemarketer. I saw you at the repair shop this morning."

"How did you get my number?"

"I peeked at the computer. I'm the thin guy with blond hair who was waiting behind you. You have great energy. I had to call you."

"That sleazy stunt could get you killed, if you try it on the wrong person."

"I'm sorry."

While Steve waited to see if she would answer, he heard several dogs barking in the background on the phone. She didn't say anything. But she didn't hang up.

"If you're not too freaked out...maybe we could get a cup of coffee."

"If you're a creep, you'll regret this call. I'm not some defenseless piece of fluff."

"Fair enough. You could probably beat the crap out of me anyway. I'm not much of a fighter."

A week later, the homeless guy was still there. Steve had named him Boris.

"Fuck you," Boris yelled every day, despite Steve's efforts to open the gate silently and tiptoe out to savor the beauty of the canal.

One day Steve was wheeling his garbage can out to the alley when his neighbor's red 1978 Pacer pulled out of its garage. Hal, somewhere in his sixties with long white hair and a beard, was dressed in a fancy square dance outfit, colorful shirt and suspenders. He waved and rolled down his window when Steve approached.

Steve mentioned the stranger in front of Hal's house.

"He's not a stranger. I met him years ago. Kind of feel sorry for him. I don't think he'll be here much longer."

Steve's mind raced, imagining scenarios in which Hal and Boris could have connected. Had Boris once been rich?

Had he once owned a dog, a giant poodle that had to be clipped so often that they'd become friends?

Or perhaps Boris was a male version of one of the homeless mall ladies. But at least they could loiter relatively undisturbed. Boris, with his ragged clothes and five day growth of beard, would probably have been thrown out. Steve felt a wave of sympathy for the man.

"Fuck you!" Boris shouted when Steve returned to the deck.

"I've got a sandwich for you." Steve stepped on a chair and held it over his head so that Boris could see it.

"Shove it up your ass and let it rot there."

Steve went inside and ate the sandwich himself. Without being able to enjoy his deck and the water, living on the canal was dreary.

A contractor was working on the house on the other side of Steve's yard. A couple in their fifties had bought the place a year earlier. They'd married recently, after living together for nine years, and were having an addition built. A squad of short, Spanish-speaking laborers were chipping away at the old foundation and digging a trench for a new footing wall.

Steve watched them from his bathroom window while he was shaving. Marty had agreed to meet him at a coffee house in the San Fernando Valley. He was already late and hurrying to get dressed when he heard knocking. Steve opened the alley door. A bull of a guy with a round face and a wide moustache held out his calloused hand.

"Tony Garcia. Sorry to bother you. I'm the contractor working next door." Garcia shifted from foot to foot nervously, like a kid putting off going to the bathroom.

"Yeah?"

"Have you lived here long?"

"A few years." Steve tucked in his shirt and buttoned his cuffs. "Why?"

"Because my men talked to a couple of maids down the block and they heard stories that a body was discovered in the foundation of the house when it was remodeled ten years ago. They're saying they're afraid to work there."

"I'm sure if there was a body, the police would have taken it away."

"But do you *know* that they did that?"

"I really don't know anything about it. Sorry."

Steve had heard the story, but had always assumed it was just a bit of exotic neighborhood lore.

The contractor went back to the other yard. He spoke to his crew, and they resumed their work.

While Steve was putting on his coat, he detected a strange odor, like a decomposing body. "Power of suggestion," he said as he opened the front door to look for a second at the unused canoe.

"Fuck you," Boris shouted.

A rotten beef taco sailed over the fence and landed at Steve's feet.

The coffee date with Marty ended up pretty well, considering that she arrived almost an hour late. Steve had grown more indignant by the minute and was on the point of walking out when she hurried in and flopped down across from him.

"Sorry, sorry." She fidgeted in her seat, brushing bits of lint off her shoulder. Her jeans jacket was shredded on one arm; blood spotted her pant legs. Steve was disappointed that she hadn't dressed up a little.

"You get attacked by one of your dogs?" he asked.

"A black leopard, actually."

"You're kidding."

"Not attacked. He just decided to bite. Big cats do that sometimes. So I let him hold my arm in his teeth for a moment and then he let it go. But it took me a long time to get him back into his pen."

She smoothed her jacket, pulled a couple of loose threads off the ripped area and shrugged. "So what have you been doing?"

He didn't know what to say. He had been prepared to impress her with the dangers and adventures of living next to Boris and with the rumor about a dead body buried in concrete, but the Boris business seemed tame compared to her life, and talking about a dead body didn't feel like the best intro to a first date. "Not much," he told her.

While he was buying her a mocha latte he tried to think of something interesting to say. But nothing came to him. He returned to the table with lattes and scones.

"So," she said, sipping hers and rimming her upper lip in foam. "Have you been peeking into women's purses? Stalking secretaries? Calling random names from the phone book?"

"If you want the truth, I haven't been doing anything very exciting. I'd like to tell you I've had some big adventure. But the one little drama I've been dealing with has kind of intimidated me. I'm sorry I can't make my life seem more exciting."

"Don't be. I meet so many guys who hear what I do and immediately try to compete to prove that they're braver or more macho or more successful than I am, that's it's a relief to find one who can be a schlumpf without worrying about it." He looked hurt. She punched his shoulder. "Just kidding. I'm sure you have lots of interesting things in your life."

He nodded offhandedly, as if to confirm her statement, but he couldn't think of anything interesting. He brokered commercial real estate and did pretty well at it, but his daily routine was hardly fodder for sparkling conversation.

He decided to concentrate on listening, which worked out well because she wanted to talk. She told him she worked for a religious cult that had bought a bunch of exotic animals and didn't know what to do with them. The group's leader was an ex-narcotics cop, a woman who had managed to steal enough money from the drug dealers to buy herself two hundred acres in the Santa Ynez valley and start her own little wildlife compound.

As Marty talked, Steve found himself looking at her teeth—her canines, in fact. They were longer than normal, and he mused for a while on whether they had grown in sympathy to the big cats she tended or whether she was actually a "cat woman." The image of Michelle Pfeiffer with whiskers and a tail flashed through his mind.

He pictured Marty walking with him to the car, pausing while he said good night, then turning and sinking her fangs into his neck the way female cheetahs did, closing off his windpipe until he suffocated.

Marty was describing a pack of hyenas that Lena, the ex-cop-cult-leader, had brought back from Africa. They had escaped and hunted down the neighbor's cattle until Marty brought them in.

Her bravado and mystery entranced him. He didn't even know her, yet he felt that her spirit had intertwined with his. That's probably how she handles the cats, he thought. Maybe she's stitching me into her life without me knowing it, making a quilt of me and the animals.

Apparently Boris had been doing some stitching of his own. As soon as Steve stepped onto his deck later that night, a dead rat, tied to a dirty Lakers cap, sailed over the fence and bounced off Steve's chest.

The shock erased his inhibitions about confronting Boris. He shouted, "If you throw any more dead animals in my yard, I'll have you locked away."

"Fuck you!"

"I'm not kidding."

"*You're* a dead animal."

The smell of decaying flesh assaulted Steve as he stepped inside the house. He was tired, but he knew he'd have to find its source. He checked the kitchen, the bathroom, the pantry, and the sun porch. But the odor didn't get any stronger there. Finally he pulled down the spring-loaded ladder leading to the attic. As soon as he pushed his head above the ceiling, the odor made him gag. He got a clothespin, put it over his nose and went back up with a flashlight.

It took him half an hour to find the source of the stench—a possum caught beneath the floorboards of the attic. It was stiff, lying on its back, its little scaled feet curled up as if it were begging for a treat. A smattering of thick hairs covered its body. It had a rat snout and a rat-like tail with scales that looked like a frozen conga line of tiny shelled animals. Steve thought of the chicken feet offerings he'd seen in dim sum restaurants, and shuddered. Even with the clothespin on his nose, the smell was overpowering. Steve got his fireplace tongs, picked up the dead possum and stuffed it into a plastic bag. He considered throwing it over the fence at Boris. But he knew that it would return in some more unpleasant fashion, so he tossed the bag into the garbage can.

"Eat shit," Boris said as Steve went back inside.

The next morning, awakened by a racket in front of his house, Steve opened the window and heard Boris shouting at someone.

"Shut that fucking thing up or I'm going to strangle it," Boris screamed from beyond the ivy. "I'll roast it and cook it for dinner."

"Aawwwwkkk!" came the reply.

"Shut up!"

Steve peeked out his front gate. He saw a giant green parrot in a tree in the yard on the far side of Hal's front gate.

"Awwwwkkk!" the parrot screeched.

Steve smiled and sauntered into the house, pleased with the thought that Boris had another target for his wrath.

The parrot and Boris seemed to settle down for a while. Steve spent the afternoon cleaning his house. He had invited Marty over for dinner and wanted to make the place look as nice as possible. He bought a bouquet of flowers for the dining room table, then picked half a dozen tomatoes and sprigs of basil from the plants on his deck. He selected several CDs—an early Charlie Byrd, a Mongo Santamaria, and a couple of light jazz piano collections by Keith Jarrett. He started the barbecue fire early so that the coals would be glowing softly for the Copper River salmon.

As if in competition, Boris had started a crude wood fire of his own on the other side of the ivy. The smoke curled over the fence.

Boris and the parrot were in battle mode.

"Aawwwkkkk! Awwwwwkkkk!" the parrot shrieked.

"Shut the fuck up!" Boris replied.

"Shut the fuck up! Awwwkkkk!" squawked the parrot.

"Oh my God," Marty said when she stepped into the yard.

"Don't pay any attention," Steve tried to lead her back inside. "It's that crazy homeless guy I told you about. He's arguing with a parrot from across the sidewalk."

"Awwwwwkk! Awwwkkk!"

"Shut up! Shut up! I'll wring your fucking neck."

Marty turned away from Steve and bolted out the gate. He ran after her. "If you confront him, he just gets worse."

"I don't give a shit," she said. "I'm not letting him hurt that bird."

"They're just arguing."

"The hell they are!"

She pushed through Hal's gate, Steve right behind her. Standing in the front yard beside a campfire with a spit suspended above it, Boris struggled with one hand to force the parrot's head down onto a wooden block; in the other he brandished a rusty hatchet.

"Shut up," the bird squawked.

With a movement so quick that it startled Steve, Marty leapt forward and snatched the parrot from Boris' grip.

He waved the hatchet at her. "Get the fuck out of my yard."

Marty stared at him. "You don't hurt animals."

"You don't hurt animals," the parrot said.

"I do any fucking thing I want," Boris said. "Give me back my dinner!"

He raised the hatchet to strike her. Without thinking, Steve rushed between them just as Boris swung the hatchet. It caught him on the shoulder, opening up a big gash. Steve stared at the wound, which wasn't bleeding yet. It looked like a deep cut in soft white wax.

Boris took another swing, which would have split Steve's skull. But Marty shoved Steve aside and grabbed Boris' hand, twisting it hard. The hatchet fell.

Boris tripped and landed on the ground. "I'll get you, bitch. And you too." He shook his fist at Steve.

"Come on." Marty grabbed Steve's sleeve. The two of them ran out with the bird.

Once inside his yard they locked the gate. "Awwwkkk!" The parrot squawked, flapping and securing its perch on her coat sleeve with its claws. The parrot bit Marty's ear and held on. A thin line of blood ran down her neck. Steve tried to grab the bird.

"It's all right. He's just scared," she said, and in a moment the parrot let go.

Marty drove Steve to the hospital. She called the police while a doc stitched his shoulder.

"You were amazing with Boris," he said while she was driving him home.

"Yeah, well, I go on automatic pilot when someone's trying to kill me, or some creature I care about."

"But you let the leopard bite you, and the parrot."

"They weren't trying to kill me. That guy was."

When they returned to Steve's house, a patrol car was parked in the alley. A uniformed cop met them at the gate. "We couldn't find the guy. We've got a bulletin out, but those homeless wackos can melt into the woodwork. He could be ten miles away or behind a garage a block from here."

Marty helped Steve cook the supper, which they ate in silence. She didn't seem to want to talk.

"You're a nice guy," she said when they were through. "I'll just hang around to be sure you're all right." She sat in his big armchair and picked up the book on Assyria.

Steve downed a couple of the pain pills the doctor had given him. In ten minutes he was out cold.

When he awoke the next morning, Marty was gone.

Steve heard "Shut the fuck up!" He jumped. "Shit," he said and leapt out of bed, expecting to see Boris in his bedroom doorway, hatchet raised. But no one was there.

Steve went outside, opened his gate, peeked around it and saw the parrot in its tree two doors away.

"Awwkkk," it squawked. "Shut your pie hole." Trembling, Steve tiptoed forward and peered into Hal's yard. Boris and his sleeping bag were gone.

As he went back home and closed his gate he heard the faint crackle of a police radio in the alley, and then excited Spanish voices in the other yard. He heard a cop giving orders, and he followed the sound to the construction site.

The laborers stood around the foundation pit, looking down. Two police techs were snapping photos and checking footprints in the soft earth. Steve crawled under the yellow crime scene tape and approached the hole. Boris lay stretched out on his back, mouth and eyes wide open. There was blood on his chest and what looked like two big puncture wounds in his neck.

Steve phoned Marty, but she didn't answer.

He dressed quickly and drove to his office, where he made a bunch of calls to set up a deal for a manufacturing plant site in Hawthorne. He kept himself busy all day.

The next day he picked up the phone to ring Marty, but somehow he couldn't bring himself to do it. What he did instead was to fix up the canoe and paddle around the canals. Being out on the water wasn't such a big deal after all.

Journey's End

We've arrived at the end our crime spree, pleased you've survived the trip. Although we could only visit a few of L.A.'s landmarks, there are many more to explore, and no doubt, more murder brewing in the criminal minds that lurk in the shadows.

Therefore, the next time you hike to the Hollywood sign, or gobble a French dip at Philippe's, or stroll the lush grounds of the Huntington Library and Gardens, remember to look over your shoulder. You never know when you could be LAndmarked for murder...

ABOUT THE AUTHORS:

Gay Degani ("Leaving Slackerland") teaches English Composition at Pasadena City College, Pasadena, California. She is currently working on a mystery novel.

Gayle Bartos-Pool ("Just Like Old Times") was born in Omaha, Nebraska. Her father was a pilot in the U.S. Air Force and the family lived in various countries from Okinawa to France, as well as on military bases in the States. The family settled in Memphis where she attended college. G.B. took a year off from college and worked on a small-town paper as a reporter and then as a private detective with a local Memphis firm, taking assignments in Atlanta, Chicago, and Little Rock. Upon graduation from Rhodes College in Memphis, she worked a year as a draftsman and then moved to California where she started her writing career and then launched her own publishing company, SPYGAME Press. Married to a Texan similar to the "Fred" character in her Ginger Caulfield Mysteries, G.B. writes mysteries, spy novels, and Christmas stories.

Darrell James ("Making It With Gammy") lives in Pasadena with his wife and manager, Diana. His short stories have appeared in a number of mystery magazines to include: *Futures Mysterious Anthology Magazine*, *Armchair Aesthete*, and (upcoming in) *Hardboiled*. He is the 2004 winner of the "Fire to Fly" competition, and a prior year finalist in "Fire To Fly". His screenplay *First Hostage* was a semi-finalist in the prestigious 2003 Slam Dance Screenplay Competition. He is currently working on a novel.

Dee Ann Palmer ("Marathon Madness") is a native Texan transplanted to Southern California. She has a bachelor of science in nursing and a master of arts in health education and administration. Her latest book, *Cry of the Bells*, is an historical romantic suspense. She credits tips from a panel in SinC/LA's 2003 *No Crime Unpublished* conference with finding a publisher for it. She's sold over sixty shorter pieces, and contributed to *Mean Girls Grown Up*, a 2005 book about female relational aggression by Cheryl Dellasega, Ph.D. A runner, Dee Ann has competed in six marathons and a hundred shorter races.

Paul D. Marks ("Sleepy Lagoon Nocturne") is the stealth screenwriter, making his living from optioning screenplays of his own and rewriting (script doctoring) other people's scripts and developing their ideas. *White Heat*, his unpublished noir novel, recently took 2nd place in the prestigious SouthWest Writers competition. And his short story "Netiquette" won first place in the Futures Short Story Contest. "Dem Bones" was a finalist in the Southern Writers Association contest. His story, "The Good Old Days" will be appearing in the upcoming anthology *Murder Across the Map*. He has also had short stories appear in the anthologies *Dime, Murder on Sunset Boulevard, Murder by Thirteen* and *Fiction on the Run*, as well as in such magazines as *Crimestalker Casebook, Penny-A-Liner* and *Futures*. A Los Angeles native, Paul loves the city that L.A. was. Dodging bullets, he's not so sure about the city it is today. You can find him at www.PaulDMarks.com.

Kate Thornton ("It Doesn't Take a Genius") has worked at such diverse jobs as selling bear tags in Alaska and dressing dancers for performances at CalTech. After retiring from a 22-year career as an instructor in the US Army, she now devotes her days to national defense work and her sleepless nights to writing stories. With over 50 short stories in print, her writing career began with a vignette of the revenge murder of someone who irritated her and has grown into an insatiable need to restore the moral order of the world through fiction. She may be found at the usual Los Angeles landmarks, just looking for trouble.

Jinx Beers ("'The Best Laid Schemes...'") wrote her first complete poem at age seven. In junior college she won a blue ribbon for a mystery in the school's short story contest. She spent eighteen years writing research and technical papers at UCLA School of Engineering. For fourteen years she was publisher and editor of *The Lesbian News*, a community newspaper which recently celebrated its 30th birthday. She also edited five volumes of *Lesbian Short Fiction*. Jinx was delighted to be included in SinC/LA's first anthology, *Murder X Thirteen*, and thrilled to have another of her short stories published in this anthology.

A native of Compton, California, **Pamela Samuels-Young** ("Setup") is the author of *Every Reasonable Doubt,* a fast-paced legal drama set in L.A. She received her bachelor's degree in journalism from USC and her master's in broadcasting from Northwestern University. After spending several years as a television news writer, Pamela earned her law degree from University of California, Berkeley,

Boalt Hall School of Law. She served as legal consultant to the Showtime television series, *Soul Food*; works full-time as an employment attorney for large corporation in Southern California, and teaches Employment Law at the University of Phoenix. Pamela is married and is working on her third novel. *Setup* is her first published short story.

A.H. Ream ("Running Venice") got her first job at a newspaper when she was 16. After working at papers in Missouri, Florida and Texas as a reporter, copy editor, page designer and graphic artist, she gave up the deadlines to pursue fiction full-time. She lives in Los Angeles with her husband and is at work on a novel. You can find her website and blog online at www.ahream.com.

Arthur Coburn ("Some Creature I Care About") graduated from Dartmouth College and Harvard Law School, and survived a one year law career in Seattle before bailing out to direct commercials, industrials and documentaries; and to write educational films. He later worked there as a freelance writer and still photographer. After moving to Hollywood, he has been a film editor on more than two dozen films, including *Spiderman*, *A Simple Plan* and *The Cooler*. In June 2005 he won the Novel Prize at the Southern California Writer's Conference for his thriller, *Rough Cut*. He is a member of Sisters in Crime, Crime Writers of America and IWOSC.

Susan Kosar Beery ("100 Suburbs in Search of a City" and linking introductions) is a freelance writer/producer in television advertising and promotion. She has produced national campaigns for CBS and FOX, and marketing videos for The Discovery Channel. While on staff as CBS, she wrote and produced the national on-air campaign for the original premiere of *Murder, She Wrote.* In addition, Susan has dabbled as a segment director on Hard Copy. She is part of the Sisters in Crime/L.A. team who originated this new anthology, *LAndmarked for Murder*, and is currently writing her first mystery novel, *The Rosary Maya.*

Taylor Smith (Foreword) is a bestselling author whose novels include *Common Passions, The Best of Enemies* and *Random Acts.* A native of Canada, she became a diplomat for that country, covering the former Soviet bloc, and for a time was a senior aide to Canada's equivalent of the National Security Advisor. Taylor has also been a delegate to the United Nations General Assembly in New York, and she spent three years posted to East Africa. During a leave of absence in 1990, she relocated to Orange County, California, and took up fiction writing. Her well-reviewed novels have been released in more than two-dozen countries, and have sold over two million copies.

ABOUT THE EDITORS:

Harley Jane Kozak grew up in Nebraska, attended New York University's Graduate Acting Program, and spent the next two decades in show business, starring in fifty plays, ten feature films, and a dozen TV movies, series, and miniseries. Her novel *Dating Dead Men* was published by Doubleday in January 2004, followed by its sequel, *Dating Is Murder*, in 2005. She's won the Agatha, Anthony and Macavity Awards for Best First Novel, and has had short fiction published by *Ms. Magazine*. Harley lives in the wilds of LA with her husband, a trial lawyer, two big dogs, and three small children.

Michael Mallory is the author of the novel *Murder in the Bath* and some 90 short stories, which have appeared everywhere from *Ellery Queen's Mystery Magazine* to *Fox Kids Magazine*. His stories have been anthologized in *The Mammoth Book of Legal Thrillers*, *My Sherlock Holmes*, *Sherlock Holmes: The Hidden Years*, and he created and co-edited the SinC/LA anthology *Murder on Sunset Boulevard*. Outside of fiction, Mike has written three books on pop-culture media and about 350 newspaper and magazine articles.

Nathan Walpow writes the Joe Portugal mystery series, including *The Cactus Club Killings*, *Death of an Orchid Lover*, *One Last Hit*, and the current entry, *The Manipulated*. His short story "Push Comes to Shove," originally published in the Sisters in Crime/Los Angeles anthology *A Deadly Dozen*, appears in *The Best American Mystery Stories 2001*. Nathan is past president of the Southern California chapter of Mystery Writers of America and a five-time *Jeopardy*! champion. Visit his website at www.walpow.com.